THE USBORNE
Pocket
The R
CONTENTS

WHAT'S INSIDE YOU?

Susan Meredith

Designed by Lindy Dark
Illustrated by Kuo Kang Chen, Colin King and Peter Wingham

Revised by Philippa Wingate
With thanks to Katarina Dragoslavić and Rosie Dickins

Consultant: Dr. Kevan Thorley

CONTENTS

1

What does your body do?

Your body is made of masses of different parts. Each part has its own important job to do. All the parts have to work correctly together to keep you alive and healthy.

Even when you are doing something quite straightforward, like playing, lots and lots of complicated things are going on inside your body.

Your brain tells all the different parts of you what to do.

You listen to the sounds around you using your ears. Your ears also help you to keep your balance.

Your muscles make you move so you can throw and catch a ball.

Your eyes work hard watching the ball carefully.

Sometimes your muscles start to ache. This tells you it is time for a rest.

Feelers in your body, called nerves, tell you what your body is doing and what is happening to it.

Your mouth shapes sounds into words when you talk.

If you fall and graze your knee, a few drops of blood may spill out, but your body soon heals itself.

Your body has a framework of bones which helps it to keep its shape whatever you are doing.

2

If you have been sweating a lot, you may feel thirsty.

If it is hot, you may sweat and your face may turn red. This is really your body's way of cooling you down.

You can smell the flowers with your nose.

Your food and drink are traveling through your body. You may need to go to the toilet to get rid of some waste.

You may feel your heart beating in your chest. It is pumping blood around your body to give you energy.

You breathe hard to give your body extra energy.

Babies are exploring and learning all the time.

You are growing very, very gradually all the time.

Inside your body

In this section your insides are shown in different shades so you can see all the parts clearly.

Most of your insides are really a brownish-red color a little like meat.

3

Eating

Your body needs food and drink to keep working properly.

Using your teeth

You use your teeth to make your food small enough to swallow. Your front teeth are a different shape from your back teeth. Can you feel the difference with your tongue?

Two sets of teeth

Your first set of teeth are called milk teeth because they grow when you are a baby. There are 20 of these.

The milk tooth will eventually fall out as the adult tooth grows up underneath it.

There are 32 teeth in a full adult set. Nobody really knows why people grow two sets of teeth.

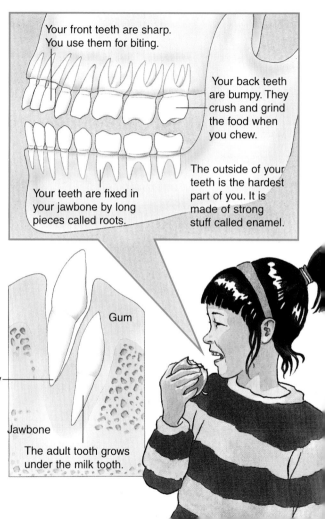

Your front teeth are sharp. You use them for biting.

Your back teeth are bumpy. They crush and grind the food when you chew.

Your teeth are fixed in your jawbone by long pieces called roots.

The outside of your teeth is the hardest part of you. It is made of strong stuff called enamel.

Gum

Jawbone

The adult tooth grows under the milk tooth.

4

Food

Different foods do different jobs in your body. You need to eat small amounts of lots of different kinds of food to stay really healthy.

Potatoes, rice, pasta, bread and sweet foods give you energy.

Milk, cheese and yogurt make your bones and teeth strong.

Foods such as meat, fish and eggs make you grow and help to repair your body.

Fruit and vegetables have vitamins in them. These keep your body working efficiently.

Brushing teeth

It is important to brush your teeth well, especially last thing at night.

Tiny pieces of food and drink stick to your teeth even though you cannot feel them.

If the pieces are left on your teeth, chemicals called acids are made. The acids make holes in your teeth.

Where your food goes

Before your body can use the food you eat, it has to be changed into microscopically tiny pieces inside you. It has to be so small it can get into your blood. This is called digestion.

Digesting food

Your food is digested as it goes through a long tube winding from your mouth to your bottom. The tube has different parts, shown here.

Three-day journey

A meal stays in your stomach for about four hours. It takes about three days to travel all the way through you.

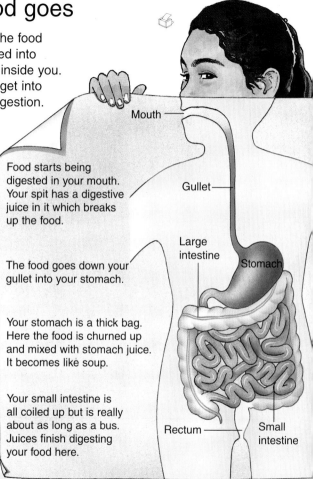

Mouth

Gullet

Large intestine

Stomach

Rectum

Small intestine

Food starts being digested in your mouth. Your spit has a digestive juice in it which breaks up the food.

The food goes down your gullet into your stomach.

Your stomach is a thick bag. Here the food is churned up and mixed with stomach juice. It becomes like soup.

Your small intestine is all coiled up but is really about as long as a bus. Juices finish digesting your food here.

Internet link *For a link to a Web site where you can read more about how we digest food, go to **www.usborne-quicklinks.com***

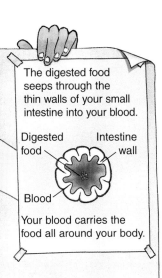

The digested food seeps through the thin walls of your small intestine into your blood.

Digested food   Intestine wall

Blood

Your blood carries the food all around your body.

Water from your food and drink goes into your blood through the walls of your large intestine.

Some pieces of food cannot be digested. You push them out of your rectum when you go to the toilet.

Waste water

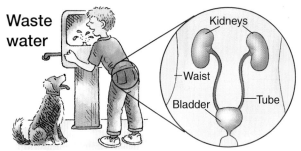

Kidneys

Waist

Bladder   Tube

Any water that your body does not need is turned into urine (pee) in your kidneys. These are in your back.

Urine is stored is a bag called a bladder. You can feel your bladder getting full when you need to go to the toilet.

How food moves along

Food

Muscles squeeze here.

Food is pushed along.

Food does not slide through you. It is squeezed along by muscles in your digestive tube.

Tummy rumbles

The sound you hear when your tummy rumbles is food and air being squeezed along your digestive tube.

Why do you breathe?

Before your body can use the energy which is in your food, the food has to be mixed with oxygen. Oxygen is a gas which is in the air all around you. When you breathe in, you take oxygen into your body.

How you breathe

The air you breathe is sucked up your nose or into your mouth, down your windpipe and into your lungs.

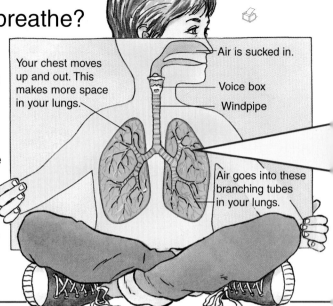

Air is sucked in.

Your chest moves up and out. This makes more space in your lungs.

Voice box

Windpipe

Air goes into these branching tubes in your lungs.

Voice box

mmm...

The lumpy bit in your neck is your voice box. It is at the top of your windpipe.

Can you feel a sort of wobbling there when you say a loud "mmm" sound?

When you breathe out, air goes through some stretchy cords in your voice box. If there is enough air, the cords wobble like guitar strings when you play them. This makes sounds. Your mouth shapes the sounds into words.

At the ends of the tubes in your lungs are bunches of air sacs. These fill up with air like balloons.

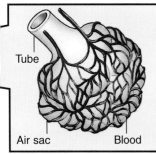

Tube

Air sac   Blood

Oxygen seeps through the air sac walls into your blood.

Your blood carries the oxygen round your body. The oxygen mixes with digested food to give you energy.

A waste gas called carbon dioxide is made. Your blood carries this back to your lungs.

When you breathe out, air is squeezed out of your lungs. The air has carbon dioxide in it.

Your chest moves in so there is less space in your lungs.

Air is squeezed out.

Can you feel your chest moving in and out as you breathe?

Hiccups

The sound is the cords in your voice box closing suddenly.

There is a large muscle below your lungs. This moves up and down as you breathe. Sometimes it gets out of control and you get hiccups.

Choking on food

Your windpipe is very close to your gullet.

Gullet

When you choke on your food, you say it has "gone down the wrong way". This is true. It has gone down your windpipe instead of your gullet.

Internet link For a link to a Web site where you can find out what causes hiccups and how to cure them, go to **www.usborne-quicklinks.com**

What is blood for?

The main job of your blood is to carry food and oxygen to all parts of your body. It also collects waste, such as carbon dioxide, so you can get rid of it.

How blood moves

Your blood is flowing around your body all the time in thin tubes called blood vessels. It is kept moving by your heart.

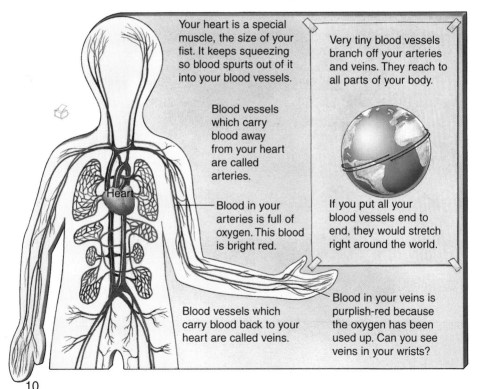

Your heart is a special muscle, the size of your fist. It keeps squeezing so blood spurts out of it into your blood vessels.

Blood vessels which carry blood away from your heart are called arteries.

Heart

Blood in your arteries is full of oxygen. This blood is bright red.

Blood vessels which carry blood back to your heart are called veins.

Very tiny blood vessels branch off your arteries and veins. They reach to all parts of your body.

If you put all your blood vessels end to end, they would stretch right around the world.

Blood in your veins is purplish-red because the oxygen has been used up. Can you see veins in your wrists?

What is blood?

If you looked at a drop of blood through a microscope, you'd see that it has lots of little things floating in it.

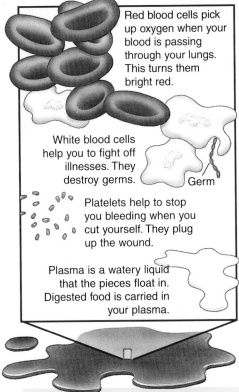

Red blood cells pick up oxygen when your blood is passing through your lungs. This turns them bright red.

White blood cells help you to fight off illnesses. They destroy germs.

Germ

Platelets help to stop you bleeding when you cut yourself. They plug up the wound.

Plasma is a watery liquid that the pieces float in. Digested food is carried in your plasma.

Heartbeats

An adult's heart beats about 70 times a minute; a child's beats 80 to 100 times.

You can hear people's hearts beating. The sound is made by valves. These are like gates in the heart. They slam shut after each spurt of blood has gone through.

Being energetic

Exercise makes your heart and lungs stronger.

When you are being energetic, you need more food and oxygen to keep going. That is why your heart beats faster and harder, and why you breathe faster and deeper.

Internet link For a link to a Web site where you can compare the heart rates of different animals to a person's heart rate, go to **www.usborne-quicklinks.com**

Your skin

Your skin is like a bag which holds your body together. But it has other jobs too. It works all the time to protect you from the outside world.

Your skin is only about 2mm thick over most of your body. This picture makes it look much thicker so you can see inside it.

Your hairs grow out of deep pits. Can you see that you have hair on your body as well as on your head?

Blood vessels bring food and oxygen to your skin.

Red in the face

More blood in your skin makes you look red.

When you get hot, the blood vessels in your skin widen. This means that more blood flows near the surface and makes you look red. The air cools down the blood, and you.

Goose pimples

When furry animals get goose pimples, air gets trapped in their fur and helps to keep them warm.

When you are cold, your hair muscles tighten up and make the hair on your body stand on end. This is what makes goose pimples. Goose pimples are not much use to humans.

As your hair grows, the ends get so far away from your blood that they die.

The skin you can see is dead because it is too far from your blood vessels.

Sweat comes out of holes called pores. The air cools you down as it dries the sweat on your skin.

Your hairs have muscles attached to them.

This layer is a storage of fat which comes from your food.

Your hair and skin are coated with oil, which is made here. The oil helps stop water from soaking into your skin.

Your dead skin gets worn away. New skin grows up from below to replace it.

You feel things with nerve endings like this one.

Sweat is made in sweat glands. It is mainly water and salt. Have you ever tasted the salt?

Nails

Your nails are a little like animals' claws. They are made of extremely hard skin.

Fair or dark?

Dark skin is better protected from the sun than fair skin.

Fair skin burns if it gets too much sun too quickly.

Some people's skin is darker than others. It has more of a dye called melanin in it. More melanin is made in strong sunshine. This helps to protect you from the sun.

Messages from outside you

You tell what is happening outside you in five different ways: you see, hear, touch, taste and smell things. This is called using your senses.

How you see

Your eyes have nerve endings in them which react to light. Light bounces off everything you see.

The light goes into your eyes through the black dot in the middle. It is really a hole called the pupil.

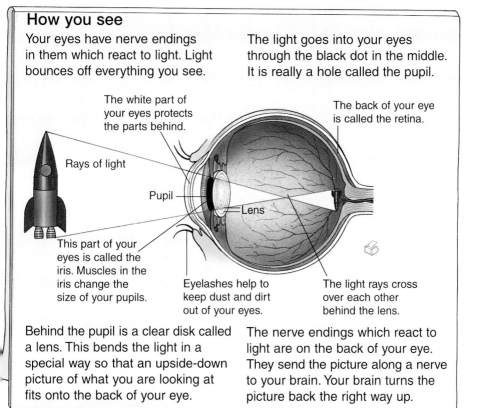

The white part of your eyes protects the parts behind.

The back of your eye is called the retina.

Rays of light

Pupil

Lens

This part of your eyes is called the iris. Muscles in the iris change the size of your pupils.

Eyelashes help to keep dust and dirt out of your eyes.

The light rays cross over each other behind the lens.

Behind the pupil is a clear disk called a lens. This bends the light in a special way so that an upside-down picture of what you are looking at fits onto the back of your eye.

The nerve endings which react to light are on the back of your eye. They send the picture along a nerve to your brain. Your brain turns the picture back the right way up.

Internet link *For a link to a Web site where you can see a movie about sight, go to* **www.usborne-quicklinks.com**

Tears

Tears are made under your top eyelids.

Nobody knows why people cry when they are upset.

Every time you blink, tears wash over your eyes and clean them. Tears drain into your nose through the inside corners of your eyes.

Big or small pupils

You can watch your pupils changing size. Look at them first in a brightly lit place, then in a dimmer one.

When it is dark, your pupils get bigger to let in as much light as possible. When it is bright, they shrink to protect your eye.

Wearing glasses

Glasses are lenses. They help the lenses in people's eyes to get the picture onto their retina properly.

Tasting

Your tongue has tiny spots called taste buds on it. These have nerve endings in them which sense different tastes.

Can you see the taste buds if you look at your tongue in a mirror?

Smelling

Nerve endings in your nose tell you about smells. Your senses of smell and taste often work together.

If your nose is blocked up with a cold, you can't taste as much.

Internet link For a link to a Web site where you can watch a movie about your sense of smell, go to **www.usborne-quicklinks.com**

Hearing and touching

How you hear

Sounds affect nerve endings deep inside your ears.

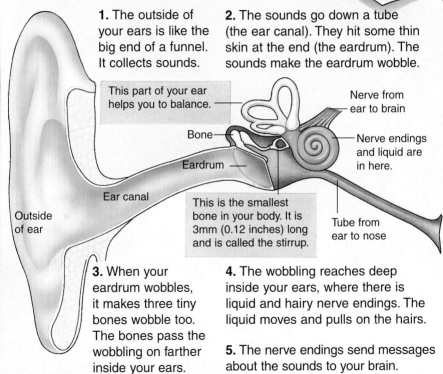

1. The outside of your ears is like the big end of a funnel. It collects sounds.

2. The sounds go down a tube (the ear canal). They hit some thin skin at the end (the eardrum). The sounds make the eardrum wobble.

This part of your ear helps you to balance.

Nerve from ear to brain

Bone

Nerve endings and liquid are in here.

Eardrum

Ear canal

This is the smallest bone in your body. It is 3mm (0.12 inches) long and is called the stirrup.

Outside of ear

Tube from ear to nose

3. When your eardrum wobbles, it makes three tiny bones wobble too. The bones pass the wobbling on farther inside your ears.

4. The wobbling reaches deep inside your ears, where there is liquid and hairy nerve endings. The liquid moves and pulls on the hairs.

5. The nerve endings send messages about the sounds to your brain.

Internet link For a link to a Web site where you can watch a movie about hearing, go to
www.usborne-quicklinks.com

Balancing

The balance part of your ear tells your brain what position your head is in.

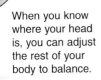

When you know where your head is, you can adjust the rest of your body to balance.

Twitchy ears

Many animals can move their ears to search for sounds.

People cannot usually move their ears. Can you waggle yours a little if you concentrate really hard?

Touching and feeling

Nerve endings in your skin tell your brain whether things are hot, cold, rough, smooth, soft, hard, or painful. You have lots and lots of nerve endings in your fingers, the soles of your feet, and in your lips and tongue.

A tiny hurt in a place with lots of nerve endings can feel enormous.

The nerve endings have different shapes.

Pain is useful really. It warns you when something is wrong so you can save yourself from harm. You have pain nerve endings deep inside your body as well as in your skin. These tell you when you are ill.

Inside your head

Your brain controls the rest of your body and makes sure that all the different parts of you work properly together. Your brain makes sense of what happens to you. It makes you able to think, learn and feel.

Brain and nerves

Your brain is connected to all parts of your body by nerves. These are a bit like telephone wires. Messages go to and from your brain along them.

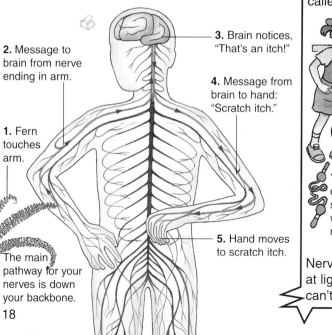

2. Message to brain from nerve ending in arm.

3. Brain notices, "That's an itch!"

4. Message from brain to hand: "Scratch itch."

1. Fern touches arm.

5. Hand moves to scratch itch.

The main pathway for your nerves is down your backbone.

18

Body electricity

The messages which go along your nerves are electrical. They are called nervous impulses.

Your funny bone is very close to a nerve. The shooting pain you get when you bang it is a nervous impulse.

Nervous impulses travel at lightning speed. You can't normally feel them.

Learning

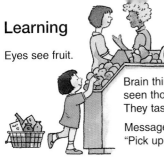

Eyes see fruit.

Brain thinks, "I've seen those before. They taste nice."

Message to hand: "Pick up!"

Your brain helps you to learn. It sorts out and stores all the messages it is sent. You work out what new messages mean by remembering old ones.

Sleeping

Dreaming may be a way of making sense of what has happened to you.

Your brain keeps working even when you are asleep. It makes sure your heart keeps beating and that you keep breathing and digesting food.

Parts of the brain

Different parts of your brain deal with different sorts of messages. There are some parts that nobody knows much about. They are probably to do with thinking, remembering and making decisions.

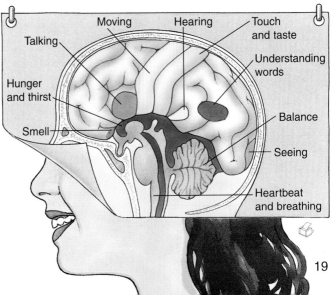

Moving
Hearing
Touch and taste
Talking
Understanding words
Hunger and thirst
Smell
Balance
Seeing
Heartbeat and breathing

19

What makes you move?

You are able to move because of the way your muscles, bones, brain and nerves all work together.

Your skeleton

Your skeleton has more than 200 bones. Besides helping you to move, your bones stop your body losing its shape and collapsing. Bones also protect other parts of your body.

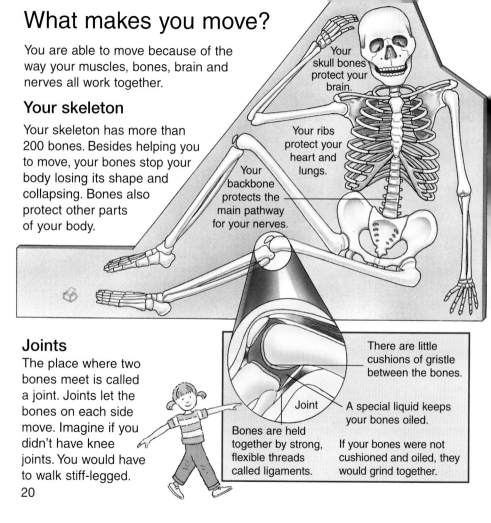

Your skull bones protect your brain.

Your ribs protect your heart and lungs.

Your backbone protects the main pathway for your nerves.

Joints

The place where two bones meet is called a joint. Joints let the bones on each side move. Imagine if you didn't have knee joints. You would have to walk stiff-legged.

There are little cushions of gristle between the bones.

Joint

A special liquid keeps your bones oiled.

Bones are held together by strong, flexible threads called ligaments.

If your bones were not cushioned and oiled, they would grind together.

20

Muscles

All over your skeleton are stretchy muscles. They are fastened to your bones by strong cords called tendons.

Muscle

Your biggest muscle is in your bottom.

Tendon

The biggest tendon is in your heel. This looks and feels a bit like a bone but isn't one. You can press it in.

How muscles work

Muscles have nerve endings in them. When you want to move, your brain sends a message to them. This tells the muscle to get shorter. As it does, it pulls on a bone and moves it.

The muscle gets shorter.

The tendon pulls on the bone.

Your elbow bends.

To straighten your elbow again, this muscle relaxes.

This muscle is relaxed.

This muscle gets shorter.

Most of your muscles are in pairs. While one muscle is getting shorter, its partner relaxes.

When muscles get shorter, they also get fatter and harder. You can sometimes see and feel them bulging out.

What is your body made of?

All the parts of your body are made of tiny living things called cells. These are so small that you can only see them with a powerful microscope. You have millions of cells.

Below you can see what a group of skin cells looks like under a microscope.

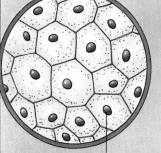

This part, called the nucleus, controls the way the cell works.

Each cell is about two-thirds water. Food and oxygen mix inside your cells to give you energy. Cells are different shapes and sizes depending on what job they do.

Chromosomes

The nucleus of each cell has special threads in it called chromosomes. These carry the instructions the cell needs to live, grow and work. Chromosomes are made of a chemical called DNA.

This picture shows part of a chromosome. The instructions for the cell are in code.

Internet links

Go to **www.usborne-quicklinks.com** and type in the keywords "pocket scientist" for links to these Web sites about your body.

Web site 1 Read all about different foods and why your body needs them, and try a quiz about nutrition.

Web site 2 Watch animations, or click on the pictures, to find out about what's inside you and what your different body parts do.

Web site 3 Lots of information about the body, with fun animated images and amazing facts to read.

Web site 4 Here you can become a virtual brain surgeon. Click along the yellow strip to explore the effect different parts of the brain have on your virtual patient's body.

Web site 5 Explore how you see, hear, smell, taste and feel the things around you.

Web site 6 Find out about teeth and how to take care of them.

Web site 7 All you ever wanted to know about body parts and sounds, but didn't want to ask. Read about belching, sweating, dandruff, snot and much more.

Web site 8 Try some simple experiments to find out more about your body's lung power, balancing ability and fingerprints.

Web site 9 Take a guided tour through the human body, with lots of images and animations.

For links to all these sites, go to www.usborne-quicklinks.com and type in the keywords "pocket scientist".

More Internet links

Here are some more Web sites to visit to find out about your body. For links to all these sites, go to **www.usborne-quicklinks.com** and type in the keywords "pocket scientist".

Web site 1 Fascinating activities to show how your body works.

Web site 2 Games, puzzles and activities all about the brain and nervous system.

Web site 3 Detailed diagrams and information about the skeleton, the digestive system, blood circulation and breathing, plus amazing facts and figures.

Web site 4 Print out a chart that will help improve your family's health and fitness.

Web site 5 Find out what makes us sick, and play games to discover how to stay healthy.

Web site 6 Here you can read all about taking care of your body, including eating well, keeping clean and preventing illnesses.

Web site 7 Take a tour of a virtual body, looking at the brain, skeleton, heart and digestive system.

Web site 8 Watch movies about breathing, and learn all about asthma. You can also test your knowledge in a quiz and read lots of surprising facts.

Web site 9 Explore some of the ways our eyes can play tricks on us, and discover how artists use visual tricks to make their paintings more realistic.

For links to all these sites, go to www.usborne-quicklinks.com and type in the keywords "pocket scientist".

WHY DO PEOPLE EAT?

Kate Needham

Designed by Lindy Dark and Non Figg
Illustrated by Annabel Spenceley and Kuo Kang Chen

Revised by Philippa Wingate
With thanks to Katarina Dragoslavić

Consultants: Dr. Frank Slattery and Valerie Micheau

CONTENTS

25

Why do you need food?

Your body is like a big machine that is always working. Even when you are asleep your heart is beating, your lungs are breathing and your brain is working. Food is the fuel which keeps all these things going. Without it you would slow down and eventually grind to a halt.

A bar of chocolate gives you enough energy to walk for an hour.

An apple gives you enough energy to cycle for six minutes.

People need food just as cars need fuel.

Growing big and strong

People sometimes say you have to eat things to grow big and strong. This is true because your whole body is made from good things in the food you eat.

Until you are about 18 your body is growing all the time.

Measure yourself each month to see how quickly you grow.

Sometimes when you haven't eaten you feel weak. This is because your body is running out of energy.

Children who don't get enough food stop growing. They become thin and weak and fall ill more easily.

Too much

If you eat more food than your body needs you store it as fat. This makes you heavy and slows you down.

Some people want to be big and heavy so they overeat on purpose. For example Japanese sumo wrestlers need to be heavy to fight.

Sumo wrestlers look like this.

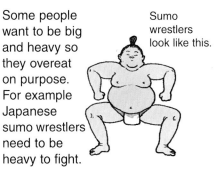

On the mend

The good things in the food you eat help your body make repairs if it gets damaged. They also help you get better when you are ill.

When you cut yourself the food you eat helps your body to mend quickly.

Water

Water is what keeps your body moist and makes your blood flow around. Without it your body would dry out and stop working.

You can last several weeks without food but only a few days without water.

Loading and unloading bread from an oven is hot, thirsty work.

Shipwrecked sailors more often die of thirst than hunger, since they can't drink sea water.

People who work in hot places, such as a baker, need to drink more because they lose water when they sweat.

What is food made of?

Everything you eat is made up of lots of different things called nutrients. These are the good things that keep your body going. Proteins, fats and carbohydrates are all nutrients. Each one helps your body do a special job.

Protein

Proteins are like building blocks. Your body uses them to grow and repair itself. Different kinds of protein help build up each part of your body.

Pregnant women need extra protein to help their baby grow.

A mother's milk has special protein in it.

Proteins build up muscles and make your hair grow.

Teenagers use up lots of protein because they are growing fast.

Meat, eggs, fish and cheese have lots of protein.

Carbohydrate

Carbohydrates give you energy. You need energy for everything you do, such as running around, talking, thinking, even reading this book.

You get lots of energy from sweet things but it doesn't last very long. The energy you get from pasta, cereal or bread is better because it lasts longer.

Climbers often carry a bar of chocolate in case they need extra energy in an emergency.

Sporty people need carbohydrate for extra energy.

Bread, cereal, pasta and cakes have lots of carbohydrate.

Fat

Fat also gives you energy but unless your body needs it right away, it is stored in a layer around your body. This acts like an extra piece of clothing helping to keep you warm and protect you.

Butter, margarine and oil are almost all fat.

Fat stored on your bottom makes it more comfortable to sit on, like a cushion.

What else is in food?

The food you eat also has tiny amounts of nutrients called vitamins and minerals which you need.

What do vitamins do?

Vitamins are like little workers which help other nutrients to do their jobs. There are about 20 different kinds. Most are named after letters of the alphabet.

The chart opposite shows what some vitamins do and where you find them.

A

Vitamin A helps you to see in the dark.

You find it in egg yolks, liver, full fat milk and carrots.

B

There are lots of kinds of B vitamins, each with a different job.

Cereals, dairy products and meat have B vitamins.

C

Vitamin C is good for health and body repairs.

You find it in fresh fruit and vegetables.

D

Vitamin D helps make your bones and teeth strong.

You get it from eggs, fish and butter.

Sailors used to get scurvy – a disease which stops wounds from healing. This is because they were at sea for months without any fresh vegetables or fruit and so no vitamin C.

Your body can make vitamin D itself using sunlight. People who live in less sunny countries need extra vitamin D from their food.

What are minerals?

Minerals are nutrients that plants get from the soil and pass on to you. You need about 15 different ones, such as salt, calcium and iron.

Water has lots of minerals in it.

Liver, meat and spinach have tiny amounts of iron in them which you need for your blood.

Milk, cheese and yogurt have calcium in them which makes your teeth and bones strong.

What is fiber?

Fiber is the tough part of food that you don't digest. It helps carry food through you and takes waste out the other end.

Brown bread, cereals and vegetables have lots of fiber.

If you don't eat enough fiber you get constipated – this is when you can't go to the toilet for ages.

What do you eat?

Write down everything you ate and drank in your last main meal. Then see if you can find out which nutrients each thing has. Use the last two pages for help.

roast chicken - protein
potatoes - carbohydrate
vitamin C
peas and carrots - vitamin A
vitamin C
fiber
strawberries - vitamin C
ice cream - nothing
particularly
good

How many good things did you eat? Were there any you didn't get any of? Some things you eat, such as ice cream, may not have anything particularly good in them, see page 40.

31

Where does food go to?

When you eat, your food starts a long journey through your body which takes about three days. It travels through a tube called the alimentary canal which starts at your mouth and finishes at your bottom.

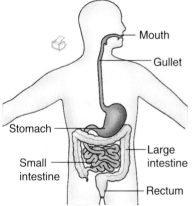

Mouth

Gullet

Stomach

Small intestine

Large intestine

Rectum

On the way, different parts of your body work on the food and add juices with chemicals in them. This breaks food into microscopically small pieces that can go into your blood. This journey is called digestion.

Food's journey

The road in this picture is like the alimentary canal, and the men show what happens to your food.

Your mouth

These men are like your teeth, cutting food into tiny pieces.

The water is like saliva. It makes food soft and mushy.

Your tongue rolls the food into a ball and pushes it into your gullet, like these men with brooms.

Your gullet

Then you swallow, and food is carried off from your mouth to continue its journey.

How long to chew?

The smaller food gets in your mouth, the easier it is for your stomach to work on. Tough meat or food with lots of fiber needs more chewing.

Eat a mouthful of apple. Then eat one of cheese.

See how many times you chew each one before you swallow.

What makes you choke?

Your gullet is next to your windpipe (the pipe you breathe through). When you swallow, your windpipe closes to stop food from going into it.

If it doesn't close in time your food might go down the wrong way. This makes you choke which usually sends the food back again.

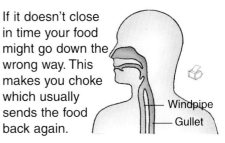

Windpipe
Gullet

Your stomach

In your body, it goes off down a tube called a gullet. This delivers food to your stomach by squeezing it along.

Your stomach is like a big mixing machine. It churns your food up until it is like soup.

To your intestines

Your stomach stretches to hold enough food to last you several hours. Turn the page to see what happens in the intestines, where food is pushed to next.

Good things and waste

After about three hours the soupy mixture in your stomach moves on to your intestines. There, all the good things in food are taken into the blood. The way it happens is called absorption. Waste moves on to leave your body. This is the longest part of food's journey.

How goodness is absorbed

The walls of your small intestine are so thin that the nutrients in your food can pass through them.

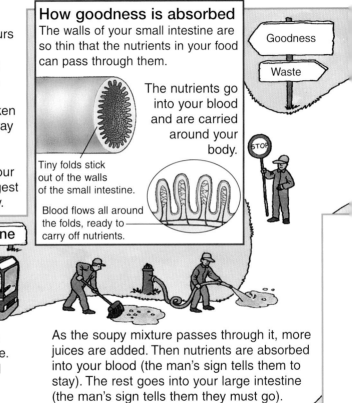

The nutrients go into your blood and are carried around your body.

Tiny folds stick out of the walls of the small intestine.

Blood flows all around the folds, ready to carry off nutrients.

Goodness

Waste

Your small intestine

First the food arrives in your small intestine. This isn't really small at all, as it's a long tube all curled up.

As the soupy mixture passes through it, more juices are added. Then nutrients are absorbed into your blood (the man's sign tells them to stay). The rest goes into your large intestine (the man's sign tells them they must go).

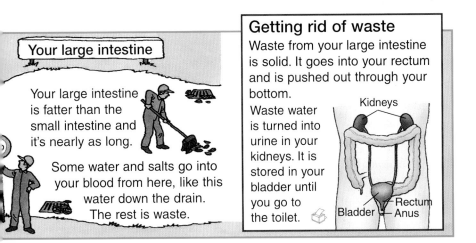

Your large intestine

Your large intestine is fatter than the small intestine and it's nearly as long.

Some water and salts go into your blood from here, like this water down the drain. The rest is waste.

Getting rid of waste

Waste from your large intestine is solid. It goes into your rectum and is pushed out through your bottom.

Waste water is turned into urine in your kidneys. It is stored in your bladder until you go to the toilet.

Kidneys

Rectum

Bladder

Anus

What makes you burp?

When you eat you often swallow air with your food. Sometimes your body sends the air back up through your mouth. This is called a burp.

Burp!

Eating too fast makes you swallow lots of air and so you may burp.

Food poisoning

If you eat food that is bad, your body tries to get rid of it quickly.

Your stomach muscles may push it back up your gullet. This is when you are sick.

It may rush through you and come out the other end as diarrhea.

Internet link For a link to a Web site where you can find out more about why we burp, go to **www.usborne-quicklinks.com**

Keeping food fresh

Your food is also food for tiny living things called microbes. These can make fresh food go bad after a few days. If you want food to keep you have to stop microbes from getting at it. They like moisture, warmth and air, so food kept in cold, dry places with no air lasts longer.

No air

Today, lots of food is vacuum-packed. This is when all the air is sucked out of the packet. Bottles and cans have no air either. Can you hear air rushing back in when you open them?

VACUUM-PACKED PEANUTS

Keeping food cold

Cooling food slows microbes down: freezing it stops them altogether. Today, food can be kept in refrigerators or freezers until it is needed.

Cold cellars have been used to keep food for centuries.

The cold does not kill microbes, so you still have to eat food quickly when you defrost it.

Drying food

Drying food gets rid of all the moisture so microbes can't multiply.

Grapes are dried to make raisins, sultanas and currants.

Today, food can be freeze-dried. This is when it is frozen and dried at the same time to get rid of moisture. You add water when you eat it.

Astronauts use freeze-dried food as it's light and takes up little room.

Heating food up

Cooking, sterilization and pasteurization are all ways of killing microbes by heat.

Sterilized food is heated to a very high temperature to kill all the microbes. It lasts a long time.

Food in cans and bottles is sterilized.

Vinegar in pickles

Sugar (in jam)

Salt in bacon

Preservatives: Benzoic acid (E210)

Preservatives

Preservatives are chemicals that make food last. Natural ones like sugar, vinegar and salt, have been used for centuries.

Look at labels on cans to see what other chemicals are used as preservatives today.

Pasteurized milk is heated enough to kill dangerous microbes. It lasts a few days.

Before pasteurization, cows were led around towns and milked on the doorstep.

Food from far away

These days food can be kept fresh for so long that shops have exotic fruits from all over the world. They travel in special refrigerated ships.

Next time you go to a supermarket, see if it says where the fruit comes from on the shelves.

Pineapple

Mangoes

Banana Passion fruit
Lychees

Food you store loses some nutrients, particularly vitamins, so it is better to eat fresh food.

37

What makes you hungry?

When your body needs food, it sends a message to your brain to say so. Then you look around to find something to eat.

Sometimes, when you can see or smell food you like, it can make you feel hungry even though your body doesn't need food.

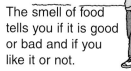

Nose smells food

Eyes see food

The smell of food tells you if it is good or bad and if you like it or not.

Even thinking about food can make you hungry.

Stomach is empty

What makes your mouth water?

When you see or smell food you like, your body gets ready to eat. You may feel water in your mouth. This is saliva, the juice your mouth makes to help you mix your food.

Saliva dripping from a dog's mouth means that he is ready to eat.

Tummy rumbles

Sometimes, when your stomach is getting ready for food it makes a rumbling noise. The sound you can hear is air and digestive juices being pushed around inside.

Internet link For a link to a Web site where you can try a quiz about animals' amazing senses of smell and taste, go to www.usborne-quicklinks.com

Tasting food

You can tell what food you do and do not like by the taste of it. Your tongue is what you mainly use to taste food. It is covered with lots of tiny bumps called taste buds.

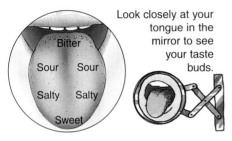

Look closely at your tongue in the mirror to see your taste buds.

Bitter

Sour   Sour

Salty   Salty

Sweet

There are four main kinds of tastes: salty, sweet, sour and bitter. The taste buds on different parts of your tongue respond to different tastes.

The smell of things helps you taste them as well. Try holding your nose when you eat. Can you taste your food?

Try this

Dip your finger in some salt. Put it on the tip of your tongue, then on the back and finally on the side. Which part can you taste it on the most?

Do the same with sugar, lemon juice and coffee. Can you tell which kind of taste they are?

See if you can fill in a chart like the one below.

Food	Part of tongue	Taste
Salt	Front of side	
Sugar		Sweet
Lemon		
Coffee		

Professional tasters

Some people can tell different tastes more easily than others. They may become professional wine- or tea-tasters.

Internet link *For a link to a Web site where you can find out all about your taste buds and just how much you use your tongue, go to **www.usborne-quicklinks.com***

Food that's bad for you

If you only ate your favorite food, your body wouldn't get all the good things it needs.

Some foods have very little goodness and can be bad for you if you eat too much of them.

Sweet things

Sugar is what makes things sweet. It is a carbohydrate, so it gives you energy, but too much of it makes you fat. It also makes your teeth rot.

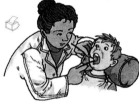

The more sweet things you eat, the more fillings you are likely to have at the dentist's.

Fatty food

Food that is fried, such as a burger, has lots of extra fat. It makes you feel full so you may not eat other things that are good for you.

Having extra fat is like carrying heavy bags. Your body and heart have to work harder to carry the weight.

What is junk food?

Food that has mostly bad things and very few good things in it is called junk food.

Candy and soda are nearly all sugar.

Ice creams, milk shakes and cookies are mostly fat and sugar.

Fast food is often fried and so has extra fat.

*Internet link For a link to a Web site where you can see a food pyramid showing how much of different types of food you should eat, go to **www.usborne-quicklinks.com***

What is a food allergy?

Some people feel bad every time they eat a certain kind of food. They may get a headache or a rash or be sick. This is called a food allergy.

One person's favorite food can make another person feel really ill.

Quite a lot of people are allergic to fish, eggs, strawberries or shellfish.

Special problems with food

Some people's bodies can't store sugar so they only eat a little of it. Some need injections to help their bodies use sugar properly. This is called diabetes.

Some chocolate is made with less sugar, and people with diabetes can enjoy it too.

Other people's bodies don't like gluten – a protein in wheat. They can't eat things with wheat or wheat flour in them. This problem is called coeliac disease.

Can you guess which things in this picture have wheat in them? The answer is on page 48.

Religion
Some people don't eat certain kinds of food because their religion says they shouldn't. Muslims and Jews don't eat pork for example.

Where does food come from?

Almost everything you eat comes from a living thing: either a plant or an animal.

Plants make their own food, using energy from the sun. Animals eat plants or other animals. So do people. The way one thing eats another is called a food chain.

Energy from the sun

You get energy from cow's milk.

Energy goes from the grass to the cow.

Bread and cereals come from corn.

Beef, cheese and milk come from cows.

In this picture, do you know where all the picnic food comes from? Can you find out what the food chain of the egg is? Turn to the bottom of page 48 for the answer.

People who don't eat meat

People who choose not to eat any meat are called vegetarians. Some don't like to kill animals and think the way they are kept is cruel.

Vegetarians don't eat meat or fish.

Some people don't eat anything that comes from animals. They are called vegans.

Vegans don't eat meat, fish, milk, eggs and cheese.

Many people get most of the protein they need from meat, though there is some in plants. Vegetarians and vegans must take care to get enough protein.

How are animals kept?

For most farmers it is more important to produce lots of food cheaply than it is to give an animal a nice life. This is because people usually buy cheaper food.

For example, hens usually stop laying eggs at night. But if they are kept in warm cages with the lights on, they lay for longer.

Hens that run around the farm are called free-range hens.

Hens kept in cages are called battery hens. They can lay about 270 eggs a year.

A free-range hen may only lay 80 eggs a year, so its eggs are more expensive.

Is there enough food?

If all the food in the world was spread evenly among all the people, everyone would have enough to eat. But it isn't like that.

In rich parts of the world like Europe, North America and Australia, most people get plenty to eat. Some eat too much.

Families in rich countries tend to be smaller so there are fewer people to share the food.

In poor parts of the world like Africa, Southeast Asia and South America people have a lot less to eat. Many don't get enough.

Families in these countries tend to be larger so there are more mouths to feed.

Other problems in poor countries

Without rain you cannot grow things. Some African countries have had no rain for several years and their farmland is now desert.

If there is a war, land for growing food may be destroyed. Often food from other countries can't get through to help feed people.

What is malnutrition?

Malnutrition is when people don't get enough of the right nutrients. This means they catch diseases more easily.

In many poor countries people don't get enough protein. Children especially need protein to grow. Most protein comes from animals. They are expensive so many people can't afford them.

What is a famine?

A famine is when there is so little food that people die. Often they die from diseases caused by malnutrition.

Who helps?

There are organizations in rich countries which send some food to help the places where there is famine.

Future food

If the population of the whole world keeps growing there won't be enough food for everyone, particularly meat, fish and eggs.

So scientists are busy searching for new kinds of food, especially plants with lots of protein.

Soya is a plant from China which has lots of protein. It can be made to look and taste like other food.

Some seaweeds are rich in protein. They grow all over the world but are only eaten in a few countries, such as Japan.

Around the world

People in different countries eat different things. This is because each part of the world has different plants and animals. This map shows you three main crops that grow in different parts of the world.

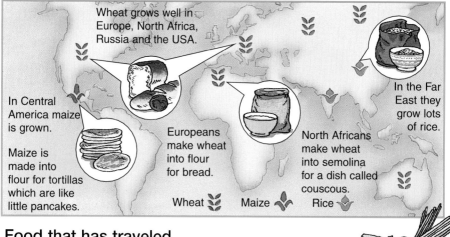

Wheat grows well in Europe, North Africa, Russia and the USA.

In Central America maize is grown.

Maize is made into flour for tortillas which are like little pancakes.

Europeans make wheat into flour for bread.

North Africans make wheat into semolina for a dish called couscous.

In the Far East they grow lots of rice.

Wheat 🌾   Maize 🌽   Rice 🌾

Food that has traveled

Lots of the food we eat every day originally came from distant countries.

In the 16th century, Spanish soldiers brought back potatoes from South America.

Turkeys were first found in Mexico.

Spices like cloves, pepper and cinnamon were carried from the East in the Middle Ages.

A famous Italian explorer, Marco Polo, brought pasta from the Far East.

46

Internet links

Go to **www.usborne-quicklinks.com** and type in the keywords "pocket scientist" for links to these Web sites about food and eating.

Web site 1 Meet the members of the Vita-Men team, and find out how vitamins help your body to fight disease.

Web site 2 You'll find lots of games to play and things to do on this site all about sugar. There are puzzles, pictures to crayon, quizzes and e-mail postcards for you to send to your friends.

Web site 3 Here you'll find information about the dangers of overeating and undereating.

Web site 4 A selection of healthy and delicious recipes for you to try out. You can also send in a recipe of your own.

Web site 5 Take a tour through the story of milk and find out everything you ever wanted to know about it.

Web site 6 It's a good idea to eat five servings of fruit or vegetables every day. This site tells you some fun ways of making sure you eat healthily, and has a chart you can print out to keep track of what you've eaten.

Web site 7 Watch a movie about nutrition and the types of food you need to eat to stay healthy.

Web site 8 Find out how to build a healthy body on this fun Web site, with puzzles, quizzes and a virtual milk shake maker.

For links to all these sites, go to www.usborne-quicklinks.com and type in the keywords "pocket scientist".

More Internet links

Here are some more Web sites to visit to find out about food and eating. For links to all these sites, go to **www.usborne-quicklinks.com** and type in the keywords "pocket scientist".

Web site 1 A guide to healthy eating, with recipe ideas.

Web site 2 Scroll down a fascinating food timeline from 17,000BC to the present day, and see when foods originated.

Web site 3 Information about keeping food fresh and facts about food poisoning. Play a game to learn about food safety.

Web site 4 Facts, games and activities all about healthy eating.

Web site 5 Become a nutrition detective, play the healthy eating game and check how balanced your diet is.

Web site 6 Here you'll find tips for a healthy lifestyle. You can also test yourself to see how well you eat.

Web site 7 Find out all about vitamins, play games and try a quiz to test your knowledge.

Web site 8 Tasty recipes from Asia and Africa.

Web site 9 Find out about Japanese food and try some recipes.

Web site 10 Information about all kinds of fruit and vegetables from around the world.

Web site 11 Test your knowledge of world hunger in a quiz.

For links to all these sites, go to www.usborne-quicklinks.com and type in the keywords "pocket scientist ".

Answers: page 41 all of them; page 42 sun–corn–chicken–egg

WHERE DO BABIES COME FROM?

Susan Meredith

Designed by Lindy Dark
Illustrated by Sue Stitt and Kuo Kang Chen

Revised by Philippa Wingate
With thanks to Katarina Dragoslavić and Rosie Dickins

Consultants: Dr. Kevan Thorley and
Cynthia Beverton of Relate, Marriage Guidance Council

CONTENTS

All about babies

As the baby grows, its mother's tummy gets bigger.

Everybody who has ever lived was once a baby and grew in their mother's tummy. This section tells the story of how babies come into the world and begin to grow up.

A baby grows in a sort of hollow bag called the womb or uterus. This is a warm, safe place for it to be until it is big and strong enough to survive in the outside world.

Food and oxygen

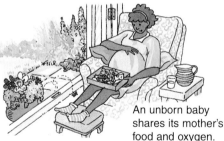

An unborn baby shares its mother's food and oxygen.

The baby needs food to stay alive and grow. It also needs oxygen from the air. But the baby cannot eat or breathe in the womb. It gets food and oxygen from its mother's blood.

50

Being born

The baby stays inside its mother for about nine months. That is about 38 weeks. Then it is ready to be born. It gets out of its mother's tummy through an opening between her legs.

Feeding

At first the only food a baby needs is milk, either from her mother's breasts or from feeding bottles. She needs to be fed every few hours.

Crying

It is not always easy to work out what a baby's crying means.

A newborn baby can do nothing for herself, so she takes a lot of looking after. Crying is her only way of telling people she needs something.

Baby animals

Kittens feed on milk from their mother's nipples.

A cow's tummy gets fatter as her calf grows inside her.

Many animals grow in their mothers' tummies and are born in the same way as people. They also get milk from their mothers.

Growing up

Babies gradually learn to do more and more for themselves.

Many animals separate from their parents when they are very young. It is years before children can manage without their parents' help.

51

Starting to grow

Everybody is made of millions of tiny living parts called cells. A baby starts to grow from just two very special cells, one from its mother and one from its father. Together, these two cells make one new cell.

Dividing cells

Each cell is no bigger than one of the full stops on this page.

The new cell divides in half to make two cells exactly the same. These two cells then divide to make four cells. The cells carry on dividing until a whole ball of cells is made.

In the womb

Ball of cells

Womb lining

Womb

The ball of cells settles down in the mother's womb, the place where babies grow. It sinks into the womb's soft cushiony lining and carries on growing.

A month later, the developing baby is still no bigger than a baked bean, but the dividing cells have started growing into the different parts of the baby's body.

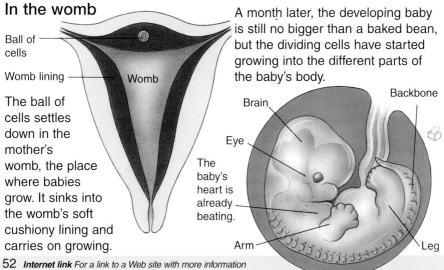

Brain

Eye

The baby's heart is already beating.

Arm

Backbone

Leg

Internet link *For a link to a Web site with more information about babies and cells, go to www.usborne-quicklinks.com*

The baby's lifeline

The baby is attached to the lining of the womb by a special cord. The food and oxygen the baby needs go from its mother's blood down the cord and into the baby's body.

Like everybody else the baby needs to get rid of waste. This goes down the cord from the baby's blood into its mother's blood. Her body gets rid of it when she goes to the toilet.

Blood vessels

This is called the placenta. It grows on the lining of the womb.

The cord is called the umbilical cord.

The placenta is where food and oxygen, and waste, pass between the mother's blood and the baby's.

The baby floats in a bag of special water. This cushions it from knocks.

The baby can't drown in the water because it doesn't need to breathe until it is born.

Getting bigger

The baby continues to grow. It moves and kicks, and also sleeps. It can hear its mother's heart beating and noises from outside her body too. Some babies even get hiccups.

Eventually, most babies settle into an upside-down position in the womb.

Some babies suck their thumbs.

53

What is it like being pregnant?

When a mother has a baby growing inside her, it is called being pregnant. While she is pregnant, her body changes in all sorts of ways.

Check-ups

The mother has regular check-ups to make sure she and the baby are healthy. These are given by an obstetrician or doctor. An obstetrician is someone who looks after pregnant mothers.

The mother is weighed. She should put on weight as the baby grows.

The mother's blood and urine (pee) are tested. This helps the doctor tell if the mother and baby are well.

Looking after herself

The mother has to take special care of herself. If she is well, the baby is more likely to be healthy too.

It's not good for the baby if the mother smokes, drinks alcohol or takes certain medicines.

She is feeding her baby as well as herself, so she has to eat healthy food.

The mother's body has to work harder than usual, giving the baby what it needs. She has to rest more.

Gentle exercise pumps more blood through to the baby and makes the mother feel better too.

When the mother's tummy gets big, she should not carry heavy things. She may strain her back.

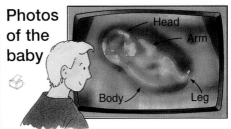

The doctor feels the mother's tummy. This gives her an idea of the baby's size and position.

She listens to the baby's heart through a special stethoscope. She puts it on the mother's tummy.

Photos of the baby

A machine called an ultrasound scanner takes moving pictures of the baby in the womb. These appear on a television screen and show everyone how the baby is developing.

Kicking

After about five months, the mother feels the baby moving. Later, it will kick.

You may feel the kicks if you put your hand on the mother's tummy.

Eventually the mother can see her tummy moving and even guess whether a bump is a hand or a foot.

Getting bigger

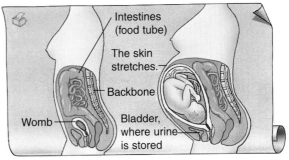

Intestines (food tube)

The skin stretches.

Backbone

Womb

Bladder, where urine is stored

The mother's womb is normally the size of a small pear. As the baby grows, the womb stretches and other things in her body get squashed up. This can be a bit uncomfortable but everything goes back to normal later.

55

Mothers and fathers

The special cells from the mother and father which make a baby start to grow are the sex cells. They are different from each other.

Egg cells

The mother's sex cell is called an egg cell or ovum. She has lots of egg cells stored in her body, near her womb.

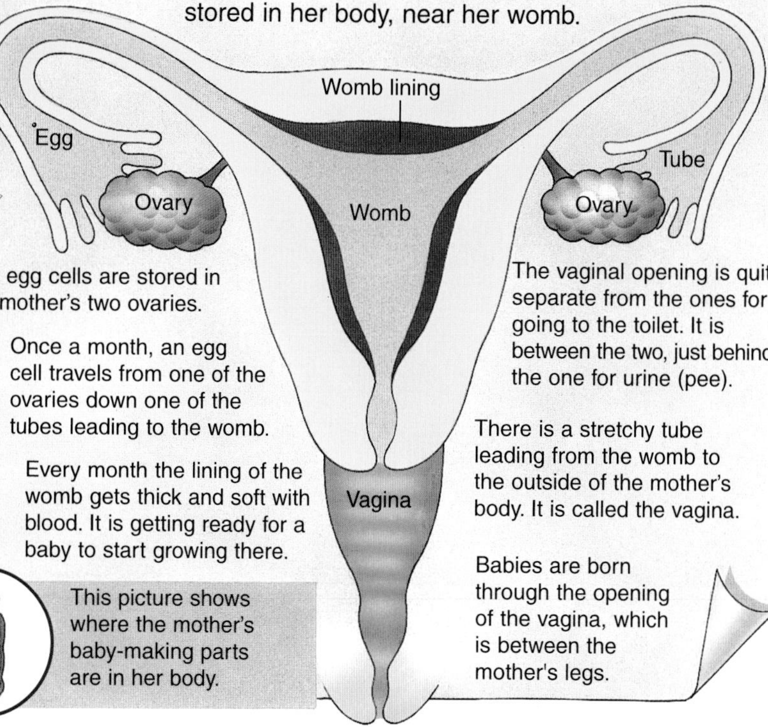

Womb lining

Egg

Ovary

Womb

Tube

Ovary

The egg cells are stored in the mother's two ovaries.

Once a month, an egg cell travels from one of the ovaries down one of the tubes leading to the womb.

Every month the lining of the womb gets thick and soft with blood. It is getting ready for a baby to start growing there.

Vagina

The vaginal opening is quite separate from the ones for going to the toilet. It is between the two, just behind the one for urine (pee).

There is a stretchy tube leading from the womb to the outside of the mother's body. It is called the vagina.

Babies are born through the opening of the vagina, which is between the mother's legs.

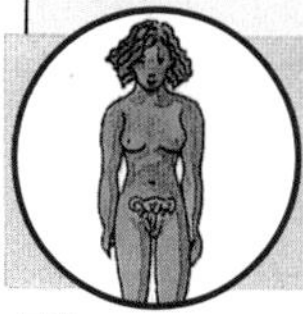

This picture shows where the mother's baby-making parts are in her body.

Sperm

The father's sex cell is called a sperm cell. Sperm are made in the father's two testicles. The testicles are in the bag of skin which hangs behind his penis (willy).

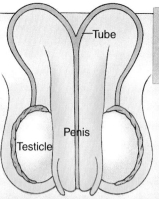

Tube

Penis

Testicle

The father's baby-making parts are between his legs.

Sperm can travel from the testicles along two tubes and out of the end of the penis.

Urine never comes out of the penis at the same time as sperm.

Growing up

Young girls and boys cannot become mothers and fathers. Your baby-making parts don't start working until your body starts to look like a grown-up's.

What if a baby doesn't start?

If a baby does not start to grow, the womb's thick lining is not needed. The lining and the egg cell break up and trickle out of the mother's vagina with some blood.

This takes a few days each month and is called having a period. To soak up what comes out, the mother puts things called tampons in her vagina or pads in her pants.

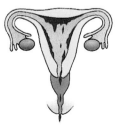

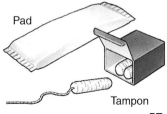

Pad

Tampon

57

How does a baby start?

A baby starts to grow when an egg and sperm meet and join together. They do this inside the mother's body. The way the sperm get to the egg is through the mother's vagina.

The mother and father cuddle each other very close. The father's penis gets stiffer and fits comfortably inside the mother's vagina. This is called making love or having sex.

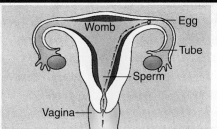

Sperm cells come out of the opening at the end of the penis and swim up into the mother's womb and tubes. If the sperm meet an egg in the tubes, one of them may join with it.

Sperm have long tails which they flick. This helps them to swim.

The moment when the egg and sperm join together is called conception or fertilization. Now a baby can start to grow.

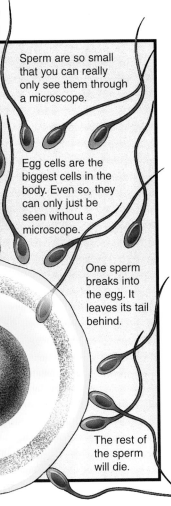

Sperm are so small that you can really only see them through a microscope.

Egg cells are the biggest cells in the body. Even so, they can only just be seen without a microscope.

One sperm breaks into the egg. It leaves its tail behind.

The rest of the sperm will die.

Pregnant or not?

It is several months before the mother's tummy starts to get bigger but she has other ways of knowing she is pregnant.

Calendar

If she is pregnant, her monthly periods stop. The lining of the womb is needed for the growing baby.

Some pregnant mothers feel sick. This is caused by chemicals called hormones in their blood.

The hormones may make the mother go off foods she usually likes; or they may make her crave some foods.

Her breasts get bigger and may feel a bit sore. They are getting ready to make milk when the baby is born.

To be sure she is pregnant, the mother's urine is tested to see if it has one of the pregnancy hormones in it.

59

How is a baby born?

After nine months inside its mother, the baby is ready to be born. It has to leave the warm, safe womb and move down the vagina to the outside world. This is called labor, which means hard work.

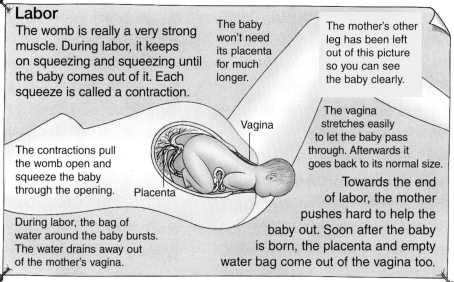

Labor

The womb is really a very strong muscle. During labor, it keeps on squeezing and squeezing until the baby comes out of it. Each squeeze is called a contraction.

The baby won't need its placenta for much longer.

The mother's other leg has been left out of this picture so you can see the baby clearly.

The contractions pull the womb open and squeeze the baby through the opening.

Vagina

The vagina stretches easily to let the baby pass through. Afterwards it goes back to its normal size.

Placenta

During labor, the bag of water around the baby bursts. The water drains away out of the mother's vagina.

Towards the end of labor, the mother pushes hard to help the baby out. Soon after the baby is born, the placenta and empty water bag come out of the vagina too.

When does labor start?

When the baby is ready to be born, special hormones are made in its blood. These go down the umbilical cord to the mother's body and make the contractions start.

The mother feels the contractions as pains in her tummy. Most mothers go to hospital to have their baby. Some choose to have theirs at home.

Helping the mother

Having a baby is exciting but can be exhausting and take many hours. A doctor looks after the mother during labor. The father can help too.

The father might rub the mother's back if it aches, or encourage her to relax and breathe properly.

The mother can have an injection to relieve the pain. Breathing in a mixture of a special gas and air through a face-mask also helps.

The baby's heartbeat

The doctor listens to the baby's heartbeat during labor to make sure it is all right. In hospitals, the heartbeat is sometimes measured by a machine called a monitor.

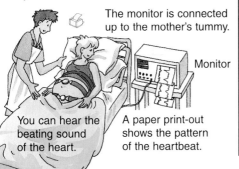

The monitor is connected up to the mother's tummy.

Monitor

You can hear the beating sound of the heart.

A paper print-out shows the pattern of the heartbeat.

What is a Caesarian birth?

Sometimes the baby can't be born in the usual way. Instead it is lifted out through a cut in the mother's tummy. This is called a Caesarian.

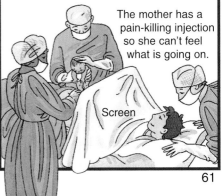

The mother has a pain-killing injection so she can't feel what is going on.

Screen

61

Newborn babies

The first thing everyone does as soon as a baby is born is to look between its legs.
Is it a girl or a boy?

The doctor checks that there is no liquid in the baby's nose or mouth. Now he can start to breathe.

The cord is cut here. The baby can't feel it.

A clip stops any bleeding.

Now that the baby can breathe and feed for himself, he no longer needs his umbilical cord. It is cut off.

Clip

The tiny bit of cord that is left dries up and falls off in a few days. Your tummy button is where your cord was.

The doctor checks that the baby is well and weighs him. He will be weighed often to make sure he is growing.

In hospital, a newborn baby has a name label put on his wrist. This avoids any mix-up about whose baby he is.

Name label

Getting used to the world

The baby has been safe and comfortable in the womb for nine months. It is probably quite a shock to find herself in the outside world. She may also be tired from the birth.

The mother starts feeding the baby.

The parents cuddle the baby and start getting to know her. Sisters and brothers come to meet her.

Newborn babies have to be wrapped up warm. Their bodies lose heat quickly.

Some new babies are almost bald. Others have a lot of hair. Some have hair on their body. This rubs off.

Babies have a soft patch on their head. Bones gradually grow over it, but until then it has to be protected from knocks.

The baby will get used to her new surroundings better if she is handled and spoken to very gently. It may also help if things are kept quiet and dimly lit at first.

In hospital, babies usually sleep in a cot beside their mother's bed.

Incubators

If a new baby is very small or unwell, she may have to go in an incubator. This is a see-through cot which is all enclosed and very warm.

The parents can touch the baby through windows in the incubator.

63

What makes a baby like it is?

The mother's egg and the father's sperm cell together have all the instructions needed for a baby to grow in the way it does.

Chromosomes

The instructions are carried on special threads in the cells. The threads are called chromosomes. The proper word for the instructions is genes.

This shows part of a chromosome.

The instructions are in a complicated code a bit like a computer program.

When the egg and sperm join together at conception, the new cell gets the chromosomes from both of them. Copies of these are passed to every cell in the baby's body.

A baby's cells have 46 chromosomes – 23 from the egg and 23 from the sperm.

Because you have chromosomes from both your parents, you will take after both of them. The mixture of the two sets of instructions also means that you are unique.

Some things about you, like the way you look, depend a lot on your chromosomes. Other things depend as well on the type of life you have after you are born.

You are more likely to become a good swimmer if you are taken to the swimming pool a lot.

Girl or boy?

Whether a baby is to be a girl or a boy is settled at conception. It depends on one chromosome in the egg and one in the sperm. These are the sex chromosomes.

The sex chromosome in all egg cells is called X. Half the sperm also have an X sex chromosome but half have one called Y.

If a sperm with an X chromosome joins with the egg, the baby is a girl.

Girls have two X sex chromosomes.

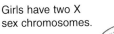

XX

If a sperm with a Y chromosome joins with the egg, the baby is a boy.

Boys have one X and one Y sex chromosome.

XY

Twins

Twins grow in their mother's womb together and are born at the same time, one by one. A few twins are identical, which means exactly alike. Most twins are non-identical, which means not exactly alike.

Sometimes, when the new cell made at conception splits in two, each half grows into a separate baby. These twins are identical because they come from the same egg and sperm.

Identical twins are always the same sex.

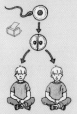

Sometimes, two separate sperm meet and join with two different eggs at the same time, and two babies grow. These twins are not identical because they came from different eggs and sperm.

Non-identical twins may be the same sex or one of each sex.

Internet link For a link to a Web site where you can discover what genes and chromosomes are made of and how they work in our bodies, go to **www.usborne-quicklinks.com**

What do babies need?

Babies need to have everything done for them. They have to be fed and kept warm, comfortable and clean.

They need lots of love and attention, and they need interesting things going on around them.

Breast-feeding

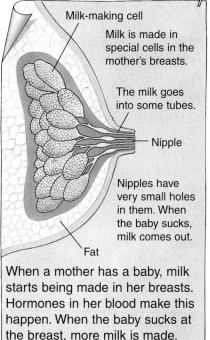

Milk-making cell

Milk is made in special cells in the mother's breasts.

The milk goes into some tubes.

Nipple

Nipples have very small holes in them. When the baby sucks, milk comes out.

Fat

When a mother has a baby, milk starts being made in her breasts. Hormones in her blood make this happen. When the baby sucks at the breast, more milk is made.

If a mother is breast-feeding, she needs to eat well, drink plenty and get extra rest.

Breast milk is made from goodness in the mother's blood and is the best food for a baby. It has chemicals called antibodies in it. These help the baby to fight off illnesses.

Bottle-feeding

If babies are not being breast-fed, they have special powdered milk instead. This is usually made from cow's milk but is then altered to make it more like breast milk.

Special powdered milk is mixed with water for a baby's bottle.

Ordinary cow's milk is too strong for babies.

Cuddles

A young baby's neck is not strong enough to hold her head up. Her head needs something to rest on all the time.

A cushion will stop your arm aching.

Babies need a lot of cuddles to make them feel safe and contented. They need to be handled gently though.

Babies cannot fight off germs like older people, so their bottles have to be extra-specially clean. This is done by sterilizing, which means getting rid of germs.

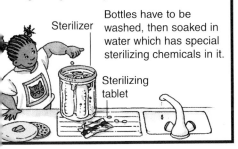

Sterilizer — Bottles have to be washed, then soaked in water which has special sterilizing chemicals in it.

Sterilizing tablet

Nappies

A young baby may need as many as eight nappy-changes in a day.

If a wet or dirty nappy is not changed the baby is more likely to get an itchy rash.

Babies do not know in advance that they need to go to the toilet. They only learn to tell as they get older.

Sleeping

Babies have no idea of day and night at first.

It can take them a long time to learn to sleep through the night.

Some young babies sleep for as many as 18 hours a day. They wake up every few hours to feed though, even in the night. Nobody knows why some babies sleep more than others.

A new baby in the family

This is an exciting, enjoyable time but it is also hard work. And it can take a while to get used to having a brand-new person in the family.

A new baby takes up so much of her parents' time and attention that older brothers and sisters can even feel a bit jealous at first.

The mother's body

It takes a few weeks for the mother's body to go back to normal after having the baby. She needs to rest. Both parents will be tired from getting up in the night to look after the baby.

Helping

You could fetch things that are needed for the baby and tidy them away.

It is useful for the parents to have help around the house at first. As the baby gets older, you may be able to help by, say, giving her a bottle.

68

Crying

A baby's crying is hard to ignore. This is useful for the baby: it makes people look after him. Babies cry for various reasons. Nobody really knows why some cry more than others.

Is the baby hungry? Is he uncomfortable or in pain? Is he too hot or too cold, bored, tired, lonely or frightened?

Babies cannot wait for things. They have not learned to think about other people's feelings and if they do have to wait long for something like food, they may even become unwell.

Brothers and sisters can sometimes feel left out.

Playing with a baby

A new baby will not be able to play with you for some time but she may soon start to enjoy watching you play nearby. Once you start to play with her, try to move and speak gently so you don't startle her. Give her plenty of time to react to things and remember that babies cannot concentrate for long. Never do anything she is not happy about.

Babies can only see clearly about 25cm (10in) from their nose.

Babies learn about things by putting them in their mouth, so always ask a grown-up if they are safe.

For the first few weeks, a baby probably has enough to do just getting used to her new surroundings. But she will soon start needing lots of things to look at and listen to.

When babies first learn to hold things, they like being given lots of different things to examine. However, they drop them very easily and don't know how to pick them up again.

Once the baby can sit up, he will be able to play with toys more easily.

Once he can crawl, you can give him things that roll.

Internet link For a link to a Web site where you can learn more about newborn babies and what it's like to have a new baby in the family, go to **www.usborne-quicklinks.com**

Babies in nature

Other babies are made, like people, by a mother and a father. In nature, when parents come together so that their sex cells can meet, it is called mating. The moment when the cells join together is called fertilization.

Animals

Animals have their babies in a very similar way to people. During mating, sperm swim towards eggs inside the mother's body. If sperm fertilize the eggs, babies grow in the mother's womb. They are born through her vagina and feed on her milk.

Most animals have more than one baby at a time.

Puppies stay in their mother's womb for nine weeks.

Birds

Baby birds grow outside their mother's body instead of inside. After mating, the mother bird lays her fertilized eggs. Babies grow in the eggs so long as the parents keep them warm by sitting on them.

A growing chick

The chick gets its food from the egg yolk.

Yolk

Air passes through the egg shell so the chick can breathe.

When the chick is ready to be born, it cracks open the egg shell with its beak and hatches out.

Eggs that we eat are unfertilized eggs. Chicks could not have grown in them.

Internet link For a link to a Web site where you can find out the names for over a hundred types of animals and their babies, go to **www.usborne-quicklinks.com**

Insects

Insects lay eggs after mating and fertilization. Most baby insects do not look much like their parents at first. They go through a big change before they are fully grown.

A caterpillar hatches from a butterfly's egg.

The caterpillar changes into a chrysalis.

The chrysalis becomes a butterfly.

Fish

Mother fish lay unfertilized eggs. The father then comes along and puts his sperm on them, and babies start to grow.

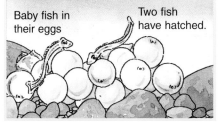

Baby fish in their eggs

Two fish have hatched.

Internet links

Go to **www.usborne-quicklinks.com** and type in the keywords "pocket scientist" for links to these Web sites about babies and birth.

Web site 1 Follow the development of baby Emma and see how a baby grows from conception to birth.

Web site 2 Find out what to expect on the first day of a baby's life. This site explains what the new baby will look like, what it will be able to do and what the experience will be like for the new parents.

Web site 3 Find out more about how your body reproduces (makes copies of itself).

Web site 4 Watch a movie about where babies come from.

For links to all these sites, go to www.usborne-quicklinks.com and type in the keywords "pocket scientist".

More Internet links

Here are some more Web sites to visit to find out about babies and birth. For links to all these sites, go to **www.usborne-quicklinks.com** and type in the keywords "pocket scientist".

Web site 1 Watch a movie explaining how our genes define the way we are, and why we look like our parents.

Web site 2 Find out all about genes and how they work. Discover how problems with genes can lead to illnesses.

Web site 3 See the different stages of a baby's development in the womb during the nine months before it is born, and find out about the effects on the mother's body.

Web site 4 Discover why newborn babies sometimes have birthmarks on their skin and read about different kinds of birthmarks.

Web site 5 All about your belly button and why it is there.

Web site 6 Here you can find out what it's like to be a twin, and read about the different kinds of twins.

Web site 7 Do you know the proper names of baby animals? See how many you can guess in this quiz.

Web site 8 See step-by-step photographs of a chick hatching from its egg.

Web site 9 Learn about a project to increase the Asian elephant population, with video clips of an elephant baby.

For links to all these sites, go to www.usborne-quicklinks.com and type in the keywords "pocket scientist".

WHAT'S UNDER THE GROUND?

Susan Mayes

Designed by Mike Pringle
Illustrated by Mike Pringle, Brin Edwards and John Scorey

Revised by Philippa Wingate
With thanks to Katarina Dragoslavić

CONTENTS

Under your feet

Something is always going on in the world under your feet.

People underground

People do different jobs under the ground. They dig and build, or repair things under the street. They even travel through specially made tunnels.

Animals

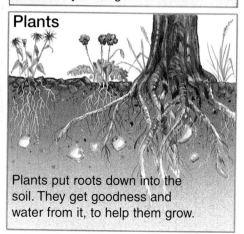

Many animals and tiny creatures live in the soil under your feet. Some of them come out to hunt or play. Others stay underground all the time.

Plants

Plants put roots down into the soil. They get goodness and water from it, to help them grow.

Life long ago

The bones of huge creatures have been found under the ground. They were buried for millions of years.

Digging things up

Your home may be made from things which are dug out of the ground. So are lots of things you use every day.

Dinosaur skeletons have been uncovered in some countries. They show us what lived long ago.

There are many different things hidden under the ground. Find out all about them in this section.

Internet link For a link to a Web site where you can play a dinosaur game and learn how scientists rebuild dinosaur skeletons, go to *www.usborne-quicklinks.com*

Under the street

Pipes, tunnels and cables are put under the street to keep them out of the way. You cannot see them most of the time, but there are clues which tell you they are there.

A metal plate on a wall shows that there is a big underground water pipe nearby.

Rainwater runs through this grate. It goes down pipes which carry it away.

Under the metal cover is a room called a manhole. Pipes go through it carrying fresh water.

Water pipes

Fresh water for you to drink and use is pumped through the mains pipe.

Mains pipe

Another pipe joins the mains and takes the water into your home.

Drains and sewers

A drain is a pipe that carries dirty water and waste from your house.

Then the waste runs into bigger pipes. They are called sewers.

Storm drains

Rainwater flows through a grate and fills a pit under the street.

Garbage collects here.

The water runs into a pipe. This takes it to the storm drain.

When workers dig up the road you can often see electric cables or gas pipes under the ground.

Most telephone messages travel through underground cables.

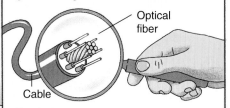

Did you know?

Many telephone cables have thin glass threads inside. Your message goes along one of these.

Optical fiber

Cable

Each thread, called an optical fiber, is as thin as a human hair. It can carry thousands of calls at one time.

Putting electricity underground

Electric cables carry power to homes, schools, factories, hospitals and stores. They often go underground.

First, deep trenches are dug in the street. Pipes called ducts are laid in them and covered with soil.

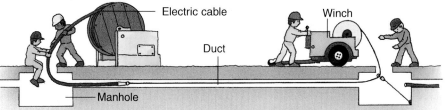

Electric cable

Duct

Winch

Manhole

The electric cable is on a huge reel. One end is put down an electrical manhole and into the duct.

At the next manhole, a winch pulls the cable through. The end will be joined to a cable from another duct.

Tunnels for travel

Many cities in the world have underground railways. Thousands of people use them to get to places quickly and easily.

Building tunnels

The world's first underground railway was built in London, in 1863.

A huge trench was dug in the road. Railway lines were laid in it and covered with an arched roof. Then the road was built over the top again.

Nowadays, this machine scrapes away the soil with strong, sharp blades.

Today, tunnels are built much deeper under the ground. Machines can drill holes under buildings and rivers.

The entrance to the "underground" is in the street.

You buy tickets in the ticket hall.

Escalators go down to the trains.

Electric signals tell the trains when to stop or go.

Did you know?

In some countries, road tunnels are built inside mountains. The longest one in the world is in Norway.

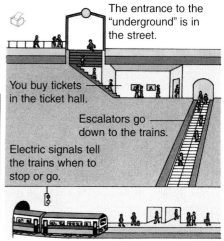

The Laedral tunnel is just over 24km (15 miles) long.

The Channel Tunnel

The Channel Tunnel is really three tunnels. They go under the sea between Britain and France.

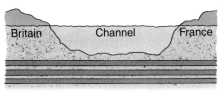

People in both countries dug the tunnels through the hard chalk. The tunnel was opened in 1994.

Trains carry passengers through two of the tunnels. They must not go faster than 160km (100 miles) an hour.

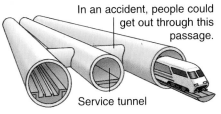

In an accident, people could get out through this passage.

Service tunnel

The middle tunnel is called a service tunnel. Workers go through it when they make repairs.

Lining a tunnel

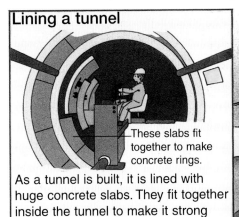

These slabs fit together to make concrete rings.

As a tunnel is built, it is lined with huge concrete slabs. They fit together inside the tunnel to make it strong and to keep the damp air out.

Building a tunnel

Electric cables are attached to the tunnel walls. They work lights and machines.

Tractors and trucks drive around inside the tunnel.

Under your home

Some buildings have rooms underneath. A few homes are built underground. But almost all buildings begin below the surface.

Building foundations

Builders make the foundations of a house first. These are built into the ground and the house is built on top. They stop the house from sinking.

A digger makes holes called trenches.

The trenches are filled with concrete.

The concrete dries hard to make strong foundations. Walls will be built on top.

Under roads and piers

Roads have strong layers of different sized rocks underneath.

A pier has legs made of iron and concrete. They go down into the sand.

Under a skyscraper

A skyscraper is a very tall building. It is so heavy that it needs special, strong foundations.

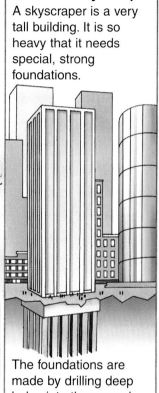

The foundations are made by drilling deep holes into the ground. Steel rods and concrete are put into each one.

Internet link *For a link to a Web site where you can see animations showing how a digger moves and works, go to **www.usborne-quicklinks.com***

A city on the lake

Venice, in Italy, was built over a salty lake called a lagoon.

In Venice, people travel along canals.

Logs were pushed down into the muddy ground under the lagoon. Wood and stones were laid across the logs. The city was built on top.

Basements and cellars

Some buildings have rooms which are lower than the street. This underground part is the basement.

This is a wine cellar underneath a hotel.

A cellar is an underground room used for storing things. Wine is kept in a cellar as it's cool down there.

Underground homes

The Berber people live in Tunisia, Africa. They build underground homes.

The top rooms are used for storing things in.

The bottom rooms are for living in.

They find deep pits and burrow into the walls to make rooms. These stay cool in the hot daytime. On cold winter nights the rooms are warm.

Holes and burrows

Many animals tunnel down into the soil to make homes underground.

These homes are safe and hidden away. They have different names.

Badgers live in a home called a set. They rest there in the day and come out at night.

Lots of rabbits live together in a warren. It is made up of groups of burrows.

Ants live in an underground home called a nest. It is made of passages and rooms.

Made for digging

Burrowing animals have bodies which are very good at digging.

Moles live in the dark and are almost blind. They have strong front legs, and can dig easily with their shovel-shaped feet.

Rabbits use their front paws to burrow into the ground. They push the soil away with their back legs.

Earthworms have strong muscles to pull them through the soil.

Living in hot places

Deserts are hot, dry places. Most small desert animals live in burrows in the daytime. They come out at night when the air is cooler.

The fennec fox hunts at night and rests in its burrow in the day.

The jerboa comes out to search for seeds and dry grass.

Keeping damp

An Australian desert frog sleeps in its burrow almost all year.

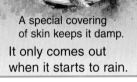

A special covering of skin keeps it damp.

It only comes out when it starts to rain.

Living in cold places

Animals live in some of the coldest places in the world. Many survive by eating a lot, then sleeping all winter. This is called hibernation.

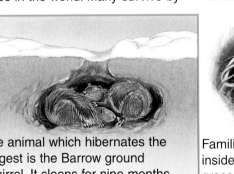

The animal which hibernates the longest is the Barrow ground squirrel. It sleeps for nine months.

Families of marmots hibernate inside their warm burrows. They make grass nests and block the way in.

Internet link For a link to a Web site where you can find out more about animals living in hot and cold places, go to **www.usborne-quicklinks.com**

What's in the soil?

Soil is really layers of stones, sand and clay. These come from rock which has been worn away by water and wind. This takes millions of years.

Nothing would grow without humus. This is made from dead plants and animals which have rotted away. The soil on top is full of humus.

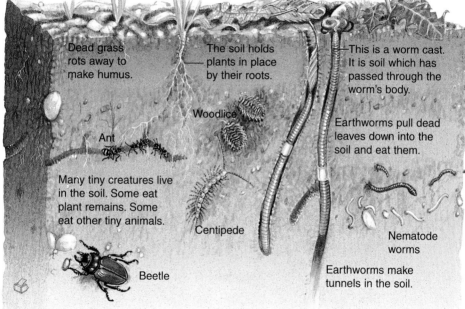

Dead grass rots away to make humus.

The soil holds plants in place by their roots.

This is a worm cast. It is soil which has passed through the worm's body.

Woodlice

Ant

Earthworms pull dead leaves down into the soil and eat them.

Many tiny creatures live in the soil. Some eat plant remains. Some eat other tiny animals.

Centipede

Nematode worms

Beetle

Earthworms make tunnels in the soil.

Humus changes into something called minerals. All living things need minerals to help them grow*. Minerals feed plants with goodness to make them strong. Earthworms help mix the minerals into the soil. Plants also need air and water. These get into the soil through tunnels made by the worms.

*Calcium is a mineral, for example. It makes your teeth and bones strong.

Making a wormery

Fill a jar with layers of soil and sand. Make sure the soil is damp, then put some leaves on top.

Cover the jar with a cloth.

Put a few worms in the jar, then cover it up so it is dark. The worms will start to tunnel. In a few days the soil and sand will be mixed up.

Wet and dry soil

Sandy soil is dry because water drains through it. Desert plants grow well in this kind of soil.

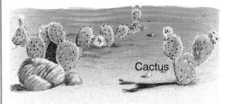

Cactus

They would not grow in soil with lots of clay in it. Clay soil holds water easily. It is wet and sticky.

Food under the ground

Gardeners often grow plants in the same place every year. The minerals which feed the plants get used up.

Beetroot

Radishes

Potatoes

Carrots

Compost heap

Many gardeners put goodness back into the soil by adding in compost. This is made from plants which have been specially left to rot away.

Vegetables grow well in dark, rich soil. The ones in this picture are root vegetables. This means that the part you eat grows under the ground.

Internet link For a link to a Web site with an interactive experiment to show how much soil there is on earth, go to **www.usborne-quicklinks.com**

All about fossils

Fossils are the remains of animals and plants which lived millions of years ago. This picture shows an animal which died and sank to the sea bed. The soft parts of its body rotted away, but the bones were left.

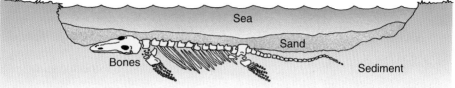

1. The bones were covered with sand and tiny grains called sediment. The sediment turned into hard rock and the bones were trapped inside.

2. Slowly, minerals in the sediment changed the bones partly into stone. These fossils were buried for millions of years until the rock was uncovered.

What do fossils tell us?
The fossils in these pictures helped scientists to guess what the first living things looked like.

Trilobite fossil

The first animals lived in water. Trilobites were sea creatures with hard bodies made of segments.

Stegosaurus fossil

Later, dinosaurs ruled the earth. A stegosaurus had bony plates on its back. Some plates were 1m (3ft) high.

Internet link *For a link to a Web site where you can discover more about dinosaur fossils and go on a virtual dinosaur dig, go to* **www.usborne-quicklinks.com**

Plants long ago

This beautiful plant fossil is over 50 million years old.

Some kinds of sediments could save plant shapes forever. There are many fossil remains of the first plants.

Looking for fossils

Fossil hunters do not usually find anything as large as a dinosaur. But they do find lots of other fossils.

This special hammer helps to get the fossil out.

Rocky beaches are good places to search. A rock may get worn away and part of a fossil is uncovered.

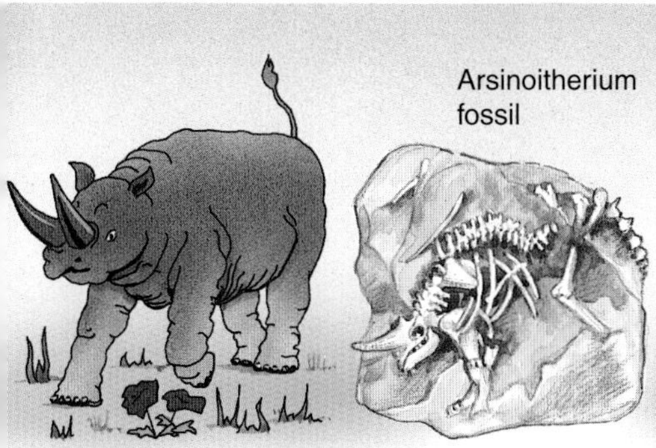

Arsinoitherium fossil

Millions of years later there were animals almost like those we see now. This one was like a rhinoceros.

Fossil of a footprint

The very first kind of human lived about 4 million years ago. The oldest human fossils were found in Africa.

Inside a cave

A cave is like an underground room. It is made by rainwater which wears rock away. Caves often form in limestone which wears away easily.

Water drips from the ceiling. It leaves minerals behind. Very slowly these begin to form rocky icicles called stalactites.

Drops with minerals in may hit the floor. They make rock towers called stalagmites

An underground stream runs through this cave.

The water trickles down into holes and passages in the rock. It makes them bigger and bigger. A cave is a huge hole which has been made.

What lives in a cave?

Most animals living in the mouth of the cave also live in the outside world. Cave swallows fly in and out.

It is darker further inside. It is also damp and cool. Bats live here and come out to hunt at night.

Deep inside the cave it is dark all the time. Glow-worms may live in here. They make their own bright lights.

A hidden cave

The way into a cave is sometimes hidden. In 1940 two boys discovered a cave which no-one knew about.

The boys were walking their dog near Lascaux in France. They found the cave when the dog fell down the entrance which had bushes in front.

Cave paintings

The Lascaux cave has paintings on the ceiling and walls. Cave people did them thousands of years ago.

The cave people made their own paints and tools. They painted bulls, cows, deer, bison and horses. These were the animals they hunted.

Try this

Do a painting using tools and paints which you have made or found yourself. You will need:

Large scrap of paper or cardboard
Water
Soil in a pot
Twigs

You could also try painting using food dye in a few drops of water.

Mix a few drops of water into the soil. Cave people used earth to make paint. They mostly used red, yellow, brown, black and white earth.

Dip the twig brush into the paint and try painting on the cardboard with it. You may need to dip it in many times as you work, but keep going.

89

Useful things underground

People dig and drill for things far underground. Coal and oil help to make electricity, but they are also used to make lots of other things.

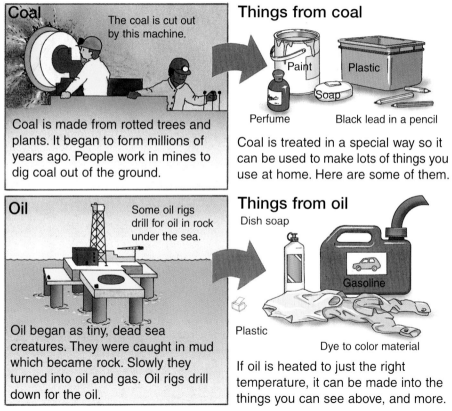

Coal

The coal is cut out by this machine.

Coal is made from rotted trees and plants. It began to form millions of years ago. People work in mines to dig coal out of the ground.

Things from coal

Paint

Plastic

Perfume

Soap

Black lead in a pencil

Coal is treated in a special way so it can be used to make lots of things you use at home. Here are some of them.

Oil

Some oil rigs drill for oil in rock under the sea.

Oil began as tiny, dead sea creatures. They were caught in mud which became rock. Slowly they turned into oil and gas. Oil rigs drill down for the oil.

Things from oil

Dish soap

Plastic

Gasoline

Dye to color material

If oil is heated to just the right temperature, it can be made into the things you can see above, and more.

Things for building

For thousands of years homes have been built using different kinds of rocks. They are dug out of the ground in places called quarries.

Clay is made from tiny grains of rock. Damp clay is made into shapes and baked hard to make tiles.

Glass is made by melting limestone, sand and something called soda.

Bricks are made from clay.

Building blocks are made from concrete.

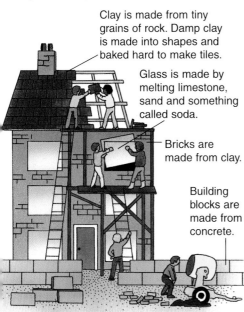

Concrete is made from small stones, sand and cement. These are mixed with water and left to harden. This makes a very strong building material.

Metal from the ground

Metal is found in rocks. You can find lots of metal things in your kitchen.

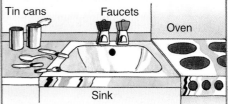

Tin cans

Faucets

Oven

Sink

Rock with metal in it is called ore. Some kinds of ore are heated in a special oven. The metal comes out as liquid ready for making things.

Did you know?

Jewels form deep inside the earth where it is very hot. Minerals far underground turn into hard crystals.

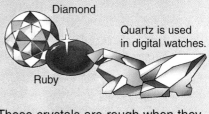

Diamond

Quartz is used in digital watches.

Ruby

These crystals are rough when they are taken out of the ground. They are cut and polished to make jewelry.

What's inside the earth?

The earth is like a ball with a hard, rocky crust. Some parts of the crust are weak and it often moves or cracks in these places.

Underneath the crust is the mantle. This is hot, soft rock which moves all the time.

The middle of the earth is called the core. The outside of the core is hot, runny metal. The inside is hard metal. This is the hottest part.

Crust

Mantle

Inner core

Outer core

Sometimes the inside of the earth moves so much that amazing things happen on the surface, where we live.

Volcanoes

A volcano is made when hot, runny rock is pushed up from inside the earth. It hardens into a cone shape.

This volcano is erupting. Hot rock called lava is bursting out of it.

This lava will cool and harden into a layer of rock. The volcano gets bigger each time it erupts.

Crater

Some cone-shaped mountains are old volcanoes. They are extinct. This means they do not erupt any more.

Internet link For a link to a Web site with a database of amazing pictures and facts about volcanoes around the world, go to **www.usborne-quicklinks.com**

Shaking ground

An earthquake is when the ground shakes very hard. It happens when the earth's crust moves suddenly.

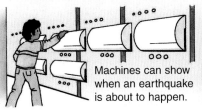

Machines can show when an earthquake is about to happen.

In countries with many earthquakes the buildings must be specially made, so they do not fall down.

Did you know?

In some places a fountain of hot water shoots out of the ground. It is called a geyser. The water is heated by hot rocks in the earth's crust.

This geyser in America spouts water about once an hour.

In some countries they use underground heat to make electricity.

Buried treasure

Vesuvius is a volcano in Naples, Italy. It first erupted nearly two thousand years ago, in Roman times.

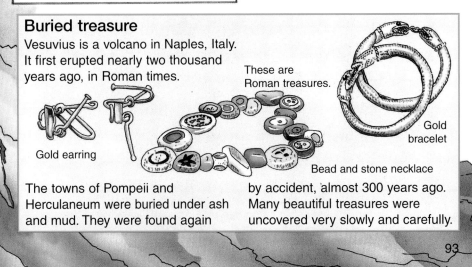

These are Roman treasures.

Gold earring

Gold bracelet

Bead and stone necklace

The towns of Pompeii and Herculaneum were buried under ash and mud. They were found again by accident, almost 300 years ago. Many beautiful treasures were uncovered very slowly and carefully.

93

Underground facts

On this page you can find out about some amazing things underground.

The longest tunnel

The world's longest tunnel is almost 169km (105 miles) long. It carries water to New York City, North America.

It is just over 4m (12ft) high. That is about as high as two tall people.

The first bird

A fossil of the first bird that ever lived was dug up in Germany, in 1861. The bird was called Archaeopteryx. It lived over 150 million years ago.

You can even see the feathers on the wings and body.

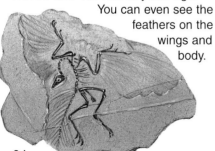

Going down

A man went almost 4km (2½ miles) down into the ground in a mine in South Africa. This is the deepest that anyone has ever been.

The biggest cave

The Sarawak Chamber in Malaysia is the biggest cave in the world. It is 700m (2,275ft) long. Imagine you could put soccer pitches down the middle. There would be room for seven.

Internet links

Go to **www.usborne-quicklinks.com** and type in the keywords "pocket scientist" for links to these Web sites about what's under the ground.

Web site 1 See if you can design a building that will withstand an earthquake. You'll need to choose the location and material of the building, and then wait to see how it stands up to the simulated earthquake you select.

Web site 2 Go on an adventure underground and see what life would be like if you were just half an inch tall. There's lots of information about the things you'll meet along the way.

Web site 3 Explore the secret world beneath the plains of North America – the underground burrows that sprawl for miles and shelter prairie dogs.

Web site 4 Take a virtual tour of the Cave of Lascaux, in France. You can find out about how it formed and how it was discovered. There are also pictures of the amazing paintings on the walls of the cave.

Web site 5 Peel away the layers that make up the earth and find out what each one does.

Web site 6 Here you'll find pictures and information about different kinds of rocks. Become an expert and then take a rock quiz.

Web site 7 Can you help to solve these mysteries about rocks, fossils and minerals?

For links to all these sites, go to www.usborne-quicklinks.com and type in the keywords "pocket scientist".

More Internet links

Here are some more Web sites to visit to find out about what's under the ground. For links to all these sites, go to **www.usborne-quicklinks.com** and type in the keywords "pocket scientist".

Web site 1 Find out what dinosaur fossils tell us about what dinosaurs were like and how they lived. You can also read about some dinosaurs you've probably never heard of.

Web site 2 Read about a caving expedition in the rainforests of Borneo, with amazing photographs of the trip and lots of information about how caves are formed.

Web site 3 Take a fascinating journey under the ground to find out about coal mining.

Web site 4 Find out about different kinds of volcanoes and how they are formed.

Web site 5 Read about volcano history, watch videos of eruptions and find out which volcanoes are erupting right now.

Web site 6 Read how diamonds are formed and where they are found, and find out about the world's most famous diamonds.

Web site 7 Discover what your birthstone is and find out about precious gems and minerals.

Web site 8 Questions and answers about rocks and fossils.

Web site 9 Learn more about dinosaur fossils by playing some online games.

For links to all these sites, go to www.usborne-quicklinks.com and type in the keywords "pocket scientist".

WHAT'S UNDER THE SEA?

Sophy Tahta

Designed by Sharon Bennet
Illustrated by Stuart Trotter

Revised by Philippa Wingate
With thanks to Katarina Dragoslavic

Consultant: Sheila Anderson

CONTENTS

Under the sea

Under the sea lies an amazing world of strange sea creatures, coral reefs, hidden wrecks and buried pipelines.

Different things go on in different parts of the sea, from the surface down to the seabed.

The surface is lit by the sun. Most plants and animals live here.

People explore the sea in special diving suits and underwater machines.

The deepest part of the sea is cold and dark. It is called the abyss.

Weird-looking fish and other animals live in the deep sea and on the seabed below.

The deep seabed is covered with wide plains, high mountains and deep trenches.

Many animals live in the sea near land where it is less deep. People fish and drill for oil here, too.

Rivers and rain wash salt and other minerals from the land into the sea.

The seabed rises steeply near land. This part is called the continental shelf.

The ocean food chain

All the animals in the sea depend on each other for food. Small animals are eaten by big ones. These in turn are eaten by even bigger animals.

This is called the ocean food chain. It begins with millions of tiny plants and animals. They are called plant plankton and animal plankton.

Plant plankton float on the surface. They use sunlight and minerals in the water to make food.

Animal plankton eat plant plankton. Some animal plankton are the babies of larger animals.

Small fish eat animal plankton. They are eaten by bigger fish.

99

Seas of the world

Over two-thirds of the earth's surface is covered by sea. Different parts have different names and the largest areas are called oceans. All of the world's seas and oceans are linked together.

The warmest seas lie near the Equator, an imaginary line around the middle of the earth.

The coldest seas lie near the North and South Poles, far away from the Equator.

Currents

Water moves around the oceans in underwater rivers called currents. Warm currents flow near the surface but cold ones flow deeper down. This is because warm water rises above cold water.

100

The tallest mountain on Earth is Mauna Kea which forms the islands of Hawaii. It rises 10,203m (33,476ft) from its base on the seabed.

CANADA

USA

North Pole

Equator

Pacific Ocean

South Pole

HAWAII

ATLANTIC OCEAN

Equator

The world's largest mountain ridge runs under the Atlantic Ocean.

SOUTH AMERICA

Red arrows show warm currents. They carry warm water from the Equator to cooler places.

The largest ocean is the Pacific Ocean. It covers about one third of the world.

Blue arrows show cold currents. They carry cold water from the Poles to warmer places.

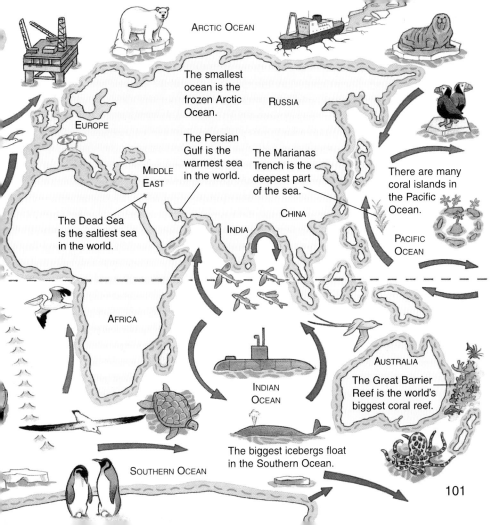

ARCTIC OCEAN

The smallest ocean is the frozen Arctic Ocean.

RUSSIA

EUROPE

The Persian Gulf is the warmest sea in the world.

The Marianas Trench is the deepest part of the sea.

MIDDLE EAST

There are many coral islands in the Pacific Ocean.

The Dead Sea is the saltiest sea in the world.

CHINA

INDIA

PACIFIC OCEAN

AFRICA

AUSTRALIA

The Great Barrier Reef is the world's biggest coral reef.

INDIAN OCEAN

The biggest icebergs float in the Southern Ocean.

SOUTHERN OCEAN

101

What is a fish?

Over 20,000 kinds of fish live in the sea. Fish are scaly animals with fins. They are also cold-blooded. This means that their bodies stay about the same temperature as the sea.

Keeping afloat

Most fish have a bag of air like a small, thin balloon inside them. This is called a swim bladder. It helps them to stay afloat in the water without having to swim.

How do fish breathe?

Fish need oxygen to live. They cannot breathe it through the air, but water also has oxygen in it. Fish have special parts called gills which take oxygen from the water.

Water goes in the mouth, over the gills and out of the gill covers above. Blood in the gills takes in oxygen.

Slimy scales help fish glide through water.

A fish beats its tail from side to side to push itself forward.

Fins help steer and balance the fish.

Lateral line

A sixth sense

Most fish have a line along each side called a lateral line. This helps them to sense the movements that other animals make in the water.

Gill cover

Deep-sea fish

Some of the strangest fish live in the deep sea where it is dark and cold. They have special ways of finding food.

A viperfish attracts fish with lights on its body, then snaps them up.

An angler fish has a light on its head. Fish swim up to it and are gobbled up.

Hatchet fish have huge, bulging eyes that point up looking for food.

A gulper eel gulps down fish with its gaping mouth and long, stretchy belly.

Sharks and rays

Sharks and rays are among the biggest fish in the sea. They do not have swim bladders so they must keep swimming or they will sink.

Many sharks have rows of razor-sharp teeth. When the front ones wear down, back ones move forward to take their place.

Great white shark

The manta ray flaps its side fins to swim. It leaps out of the water to escape danger.

Whales

Whales are the largest animals in the sea. They are not fish, but mammals. Mammals breathe air. They are also warm-blooded. This means that their bodies stay warm even when the sea is cold.

Baleen whales gulp in water and krill, then sift the water out through their baleen.

Humpback whale

Baleen

Baleen whales

Some whales, such as humpback whales, do not have teeth. They have fringes of bristle called baleen instead. These whales eat tiny shrimps called krill.

Blow-hole

A whale comes to the surface to breathe air through a blow-hole on its head.

Krill

Whales have lots of fat, called blubber, to keep them warm.

Whales in danger

So many big whales have been hunted that many have died out. Most countries have stopped hunting them, but a few still do.

104

Internet link For a link to a Web site where you can find out more about how whales use their baleen to feed, go to *www.usborne-quicklinks.com*

Whales with teeth

Other whales, such as sperm whales, have sharp teeth to eat fish, squid and other animals. They find food by making clicking noises.

These clicks bounce off animals in their way and send back echoes. The whale listens to the echoes to find out where the animal is.

Clicks sent out by the whale.

Echoes bouncing back from the squid.

Sperm whales can dive as deep as 3,000m (9,000ft).

Squid is the sperm whale's main food.

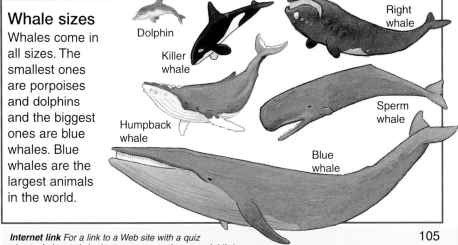

Whale sizes

Whales come in all sizes. The smallest ones are porpoises and dolphins and the biggest ones are blue whales. Blue whales are the largest animals in the world.

Dolphin

Killer whale

Right whale

Humpback whale

Sperm whale

Blue whale

Internet link For a link to a Web site with a quiz about whales and sharks, go to **www.usborne-quicklinks.com**

Coral reefs

Coral reefs are like beautiful underwater gardens. They grow in warm, shallow seas and are home to all sorts of fish and other animals.

What are corals?

Corals come in all shapes and sizes. They are built up from the stony skeletons of tiny animals called coral polyps. Polyps live on the surface of corals. When they die, new polyps grow on top.

This is a close-up of a coral cut in half. It uses its tentacles to sting animal plankton and put them in its mouth.

Most coral polyps hide in their cup-shaped skeletons during the day. They come out to feed at night.

Tentacle   Mouth

Skeleton

Many fish have bright patterns to help them hide among corals.

A porcupine fish blows itself up into a spiky ball to stop others from eating it.

Parrot fish have strong teeth to crunch up corals.

Sea anemones are like big coral polyps. They feed in the same way.

Clown fish can hide safely among sea anemones without being stung.

Giant clams close their shells when they are in danger.

Internet link *For a link to a Web site about coral reefs, go to* **www.usborne-quicklinks.com**

106

A turtle's hard shell protects its soft body inside.

Cleaner fish nibble dead skin and stale food from other fish.

Firefish stab enemies with poisonous fins on their back. Their bright stripes warn others off.

Octopuses grab crabs and other animals with their long tentacles.

Crown-of-thorns starfish feed on corals. They are destroying many reefs.

Coral islands

Coral islands often start as a fringe of coral which grows around the tip of an undersea volcano.

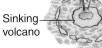

Side view

Fringing reef

The tip of the volcano forms an island.

The seabed slowly sinks taking the volcano down with it. The coral grows up to form a barrier reef.

Top view

Sinking volcano

Barrier reefs grow offshore.

The sunken volcano leaves behind a ring of coral islands called an atoll. The sea inside is called a lagoon.

Top view

Lagoon

Coral atolls have no islands inside.

Reefs under threat

Many reefs are damaged by people collecting coral and by pollution. A few are now protected as sea parks.

Icy seas

The coldest seas lie near the North and South Poles. They are called polar seas. They freeze over in the fall and melt in spring. Even so, many animals live in and around them.

Chunks of ice called icebergs float in polar seas. Some break off from rivers of ice called glaciers which slide off the land. Others break off from shelves of ice which stick out from the land.

As they melt, icebergs break up into smaller chunks called bergy bits.

Icebergs slowly drift into warmer water where they melt.

Most of an iceberg lies underwater. Only the tip shows above.

Penguins

Penguins are sea birds which cannot fly. They use their wings as flippers to swim underwater. Most penguins live in the southern polar seas.

Penguins can swim fast through the water. They leap out of the water to breathe air.

Penguins have a thick layer of fat, called blubber, and waterproof feathers to keep them warm.

Krill

Swarms of krill live in polar seas. Most polar animals eat krill, including whales which feed in polar seas in summer.

Penguins dive down for fish, krill and squid.

Seals

Seals are mammals which live mostly underwater. They come up to the surface to breathe air. Many seals live in the cold polar seas.

In winter, ringed seals scrape holes in the ice to breathe through.

A layer of blubber and a fur coat keep seals warm.

Ringed seals eat fish, krill and shrimps.

Seals have sausage-like bodies which get thinner at each end. This shape moves easily through water. It is called a streamlined shape.

Polar bears

Polar bears live near the North Pole. They are strong swimmers and hunt seals and other animals in the sea and on dry land.

Polar bears have fur and blubber to keep them warm.

Polar fish

Many polar fish, such as this Antarctic cod, have special chemicals in their blood to stop it from freezing in the chilly water.

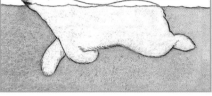

Internet link For a link to a Web site with stunning photographs of polar bears, go to www.usborne-quicklinks.com

Divers

Divers do all sorts of work under the sea, from mending pipelines to studying the seabed. Most only go down to 50m (160ft). These divers carry tanks of air on their backs to breathe from.

This diving suit keeps water out so the diver stays warm and dry.

Coming up

As divers go down, more water presses on them from above. This is called water pressure. Divers must come up very slowly to get used to changes in pressure.

Deep-sea divers

Deep-sea divers work at about 350m (1,000ft). Most breathe a special mix of gases through a pipe. This is sent down to them from a machine called a diving bell.

One of these pipes carries gas. Another pumps hot water around the suit to keep the diver warm.

Hard suits

Some deep-sea divers wear hard suits which protect them from the pressure of the water. They breathe oxygen from tanks inside.

Part of this suit has been cut away to show the diver inside.

110

Shipwrecks

Some divers explore shipwrecks on the seabed to find out how people lived and sailed in the past. They are called underwater archeologists.

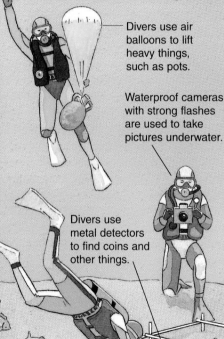

Divers use air balloons to lift heavy things, such as pots.

Waterproof cameras with strong flashes are used to take pictures underwater.

Divers use metal detectors to find coins and other things.

Underwater homes

People have tried to live underwater in special homes on the seabed. Four scientists stayed in this one, called Tektite, for 60 days in 1969.

Pipes and cables carried air, water and electricity to Tektite.

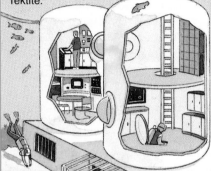

Divers lay a grid over the wreck to help mark where things are found.

This pipe sucks up mud on top of the wreck.

Underwater machines

Underwater machines called submersibles can go even deeper than divers. They have special tools to work underwater. Some submersibles carry people, but most are undersea robots which are controled from above.

Going down in submersibles

The French submersible, Nautile, can take people down to 6,000m (19,500ft). Its tools are controled by the crew inside.

Bright lamps light up the water.

These arms can pick up things from the seabed.

Interesting things are stored in this basket to look at later.

Cameras video and take photographs underwater.

Giant batteries power Nautile.

The crew members breathe air in the cabin. They look out of windows at the front.

Strong walls protect Nautile from the crushing water pressure outside.

Submarines

Submarines are big underwater ships which are used by navies.

Here you can see how tanks inside a submarine help it to go up and down.

The tanks are filled with water to let the submarine go down. The water makes it heavy enough to sink.

The tanks are closed to let the submarine stay at the same depth.

The tanks are filled with air to make the submarine light enough to rise. The air pushes the water out.

Bathyscaphes

A bathyscaphe is a submersible which explores the deepest oceans. It has a cabin below for the crew.

In 1960, the bathyscaphe Trieste dived almost 11km (7 miles) to the bottom of the Marianas Trench.

Cut-away of cabin

ROVs

Underwater robots are also known as ROVs. This one is used to repair and bury telephone cables on the seabed.

This ROV blasts a trench in the seabed to bury the cable in.

A line controls the ROV from above.

The seabed

The earth's surface is made up of big pieces called plates. These move slowly on a layer of hot rock called the mantle. This picture shows some of the plates that make up the seabed.

Undersea volcanoes are formed by melted rock, called magma, oozing up through the seabed. The magma cools and hardens into layers of rock. It slowly builds up to form volcanoes.

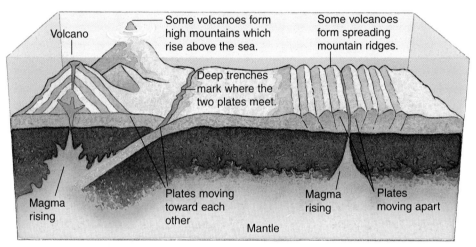

Some volcanoes form high mountains which rise above the sea.

Some volcanoes form spreading mountain ridges.

Volcano

Deep trenches mark where the two plates meet.

Magma rising

Plates moving toward each other

Magma rising

Plates moving apart

Mantle

Disappearing seabed

Seabed is always being destroyed. When two plates move toward each other, one plunges underneath. Parts of it melt into magma. Some of this magma may rise to form volcanoes.

New seabed

New seabed is always being made. This happens as two plates move apart. Magma wells up to fill the gap. It forms spreading mountain ridges as it hardens to make new seabed.

Hot springs

Scientists have found hot springs near plate edges. Here, seawater seeps into cracks in the seabed and is heated by hot rocks below. It gushes back up through the seabed in a hot jet.

The hot water collects minerals from rocks below. The minerals make it cloudy.

Cloudy springs are also called smokers.

Minerals in the hot water form a chimney around the spring.

Clams

Crab

Strange animals called tube worms live near hot springs under the sea.

How deep is the sea?

People find out how deep the sea is by timing how long sounds take to echo back from the seabed. They put the different depths together to make a map of the seabed.

A machine called an echo sounder sends out sounds and times their echoes as the ship moves along.

Sound waves

Echoes

Tunnels under the sea

Giant drilling machines can bore huge tunnels through the seabed. The longest railway tunnel under the sea is the Channel Tunnel between England and France.

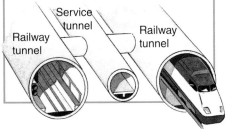

Service tunnel

Railway tunnel

Railway tunnel

Drilling for oil

Giant drilling rigs search for oil far below the seabed. Some rigs stand on the seabed and others float on tanks in the water. They must be strong enough to stand up to rough seas and weather.

This tower is called a derrick. It helps lower the drill pipe into the seabed.

Helicopters carry crew and supplies.

Strong chains and anchors hold the rig down to the seabed below.

Divers and ROVs check the rig and do repairs underwater.

Diving bell

More pipe is added to the drill as it goes deeper.

These tanks are filled with water to make the rig float lower in the sea.

The drill bit

The tip of the drill is called the bit. It has sharp teeth made of steel or diamonds to cut through the rock. When they wear out, the drill is pulled up and the bit is changed.

Drill bit

116

Pumping oil up

Once oil is found, the rig is taken away. A bigger production platform is built to drill more wells and pump oil up.

Carrying oil ashore

Pipelines and tankers carry oil to shore where it is used to make fuel, electricity, plastics, paint and glue.

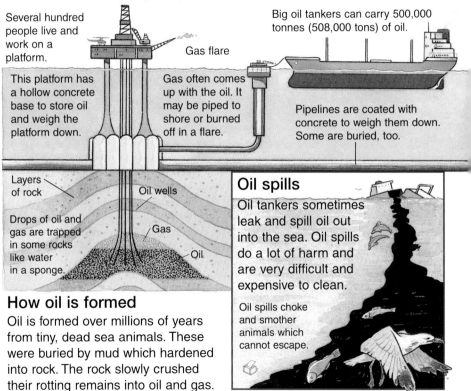

Several hundred people live and work on a platform.

Gas flare

Big oil tankers can carry 500,000 tonnes (508,000 tons) of oil.

This platform has a hollow concrete base to store oil and weigh the platform down.

Gas often comes up with the oil. It may be piped to shore or burned off in a flare.

Pipelines are coated with concrete to weigh them down. Some are buried, too.

Layers of rock

Oil wells

Drops of oil and gas are trapped in some rocks like water in a sponge.

Gas

Oil

Oil spills

Oil tankers sometimes leak and spill oil out into the sea. Oil spills do a lot of harm and are very difficult and expensive to clean.

Oil spills choke and smother animals which cannot escape.

How oil is formed

Oil is formed over millions of years from tiny, dead sea animals. These were buried by mud which hardened into rock. The rock slowly crushed their rotting remains into oil and gas.

117

Using the seas

For thousands of years, people have fished the seas for food. Today, modern fishing boats can catch huge amounts of fish at a time in giant nets.

Shellfish

All kinds of shellfish come from the sea. People usually fish for them in shallow seas near the shore.

Trawl nets scoop up fish on or near the seabed.

Some fish swim in big groups called schools. Purse nets are pulled around whole schools.

Drift nets are stretched out to catch fish. Unfortunately, they trap other animals, too.

Some nets have bigger holes. These let baby fish slip out.

Overfishing

Too many fish are caught in some parts of the sea. Baby ones are caught before they can grow and breed. Some countries have agreed to catch fewer fish because of this.

118

Internet links

Go to **www.usborne-quicklinks.com** and type in the keywords "pocket scientist" for links to these Web sites about seas and oceans.

Web site 1 See Webcam images of penguins at Bristol Zoo, England, and read fact files about them.

Web site 2 See clips from a seal Webcam, and watch a video of seals swimming.

Web site 3 Find out how sharks, hunt and swim, and discover what they like to eat.

Web site 4 Follow the clues and see if you can solve the mystery on this interactive site.

Web site 5 Watch a movie about the world under the ocean, and find out about some of the creatures that live there.

Web site 6 Here you can get the latest news on just about everything relating to the sea.

Web site 7 Find out how big the largest blue whale was, or what the fastest fish in the ocean is. You'll also find lots of other marine world records.

Web site 8 Test your knowledge of sharks with this online quiz.

Web site 9 Here you'll find answers to every question you could ask about fish.

Web site 10 Watch amazing video clips of sharks swimming, including a great white shark.

For links to all these sites, go to www.usborne-quicklinks.com and type in the keywords "pocket scientist".

More Internet links

Here are some more Web sites to visit to find out about seas and oceans. For links to all these sites, go to **www.usborne-quicklinks.com** and type in the keywords "pocket scientist".

Web site 1 All about the strange creatures that live at the bottom of the sea.

Web site 2 See animations and video clips from under the sea.

Web site 3 Find out about underwater history using this timeline. There's also information about famous shipwrecks.

Web site 4 Read about famous pirates and their sunken ships, and see pictures of things found on them.

Web site 5 Read about different kinds of sea life, and then try the Who Wants to be a Deep-Sea Diver quiz to test your knowledge.

Web site 6 Find out more about oil spills and the damage they do to our oceans. You can also discover how experts respond after an oil spill to try to limit the damage.

Web site 7 Watch a movie to find out what submarines are used for, how they work and how they sink and move through water.

Web site 8 Fun games all about the ocean. You can also see amazing pictures of fish from Hawaii's coral reefs.

Web site 9 Read all about whales, sharks, penguins, dolphins and other sea creatures.

For links to all these sites, go to www.usborne-quicklinks.com and type in the keywords "pocket scientist".

WHERE DID DINOSAURS GO?

Mike Unwin

Designed by Ian McNee
Illustrated by Andrew Robinson, Toni Goffe and Guy Smith

Edited by Cheryl Evans and revised by Philippa Wingate
With thanks to Katarina Dragoslavić and Rosie Dickins

Consultant: Dr Angela Milner (The Natural History Museum, London)

CONTENTS

What were dinosaurs?

Dinosaurs were animals that lived millions of years ago, before there were any people. Today there are no dinosaurs left.

Dinosaur means "terrible lizard". People called them this because their skeletons looked like giant lizards' skeletons. Now scientists know dinosaurs were not lizards. This section explains what they really were.

Stegosaurus was a dinosaur that lived 150 million years ago.

Giants

Most dinosaurs were much bigger than the lizards you can see today.

Diplodocus was one of the longest dinosaurs. It grew up to 27m (89ft) long. That's as long as a tennis court.

The Komodo Dragon is the longest lizard alive today. It grows up to 3m (10ft) long.

No more dinosaurs

65 million years ago dinosaurs became extinct. This means they disappeared forever. Nobody is sure why this happened. But experts have many ideas about it, as you will discover here.

Internet link *For a link to a Web site where you can find lots of fascinating facts about dinosaurs, including theories about why they became extinct, go to www.usborne-quicklinks.com*

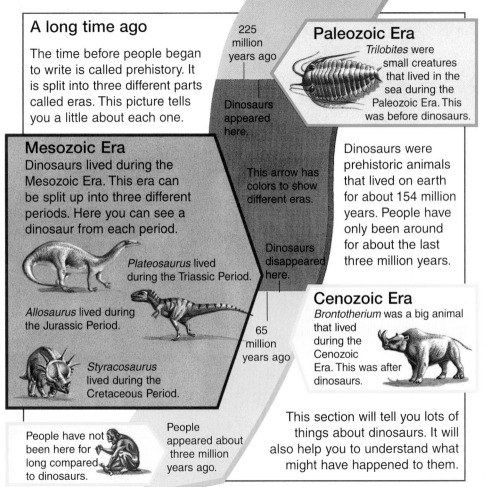

A long time ago

The time before people began to write is called prehistory. It is split into three different parts called eras. This picture tells you a little about each one.

225 million years ago

Dinosaurs appeared here.

Paleozoic Era

Trilobites were small creatures that lived in the sea during the Paleozoic Era. This was before dinosaurs.

Mesozoic Era

Dinosaurs lived during the Mesozoic Era. This era can be split up into three different periods. Here you can see a dinosaur from each period.

This arrow has colors to show different eras.

Plateosaurus lived during the Triassic Period.

Allosaurus lived during the Jurassic Period.

Styracosaurus lived during the Cretaceous Period.

Dinosaurs disappeared here.

Dinosaurs were prehistoric animals that lived on earth for about 154 million years. People have only been around for about the last three million years.

65 million years ago

Cenozoic Era

Brontotherium was a big animal that lived during the Cenozoic Era. This was after dinosaurs.

People have not been here for long compared to dinosaurs.

People appeared about three million years ago.

This section will tell you lots of things about dinosaurs. It will also help you to understand what might have happened to them.

123

What's left of dinosaurs?

Experts have learned about dinosaurs by studying fossils. Fossils are the remains of animals that died a long time ago and have been turned into stone. They are all that is left of the dinosaurs now.

How fossils were made

When a dinosaur died, its soft parts soon rotted away. But its hard skeleton was left.

If the dinosaur was in a muddy place such as the bottom of a lake, the skeleton sank into the mud.

As more mud covered the skeleton, the bottom layers were squashed and hardened into rock.

Over time, special minerals in the rock turned the skeleton to stone. This made it into a fossil.

Dinosaur jigsaw puzzle

Scientists who study fossils are called paleontologists. They fit the fossil pieces of a dinosaur together to find out what it looked like and how it lived.

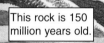

This rock is 150 million years old.

A special hammer is used to chip rock from around the bones.

Paleontologists photograph each fossil before they remove it, so they know exactly where it was found.

Fossils are found in places that were once covered by water. Here you can see a dinosaur fossil being dug out of a cliff.

45

Internet link For a link to a Web site where you can find out more about how animals become fossils, go to **www.usborne-quicklinks.com**

Getting it wrong

Paleontologists can make mistakes. When scientists first put *Iguanodon* together, they found a bone that did not seem to fit the rest of the skeleton. They decided that it belonged on *Iguanodon's* nose, like a rhinoceros's horn. But when they found more fossils they realized that this bone was a spike on *Iguanodon's* thumb.

At first they thought *Iguanodon* looked something like this.

This is the bone that confused scientists.

Now they know *Iguanodon* looked more like this.

Experts wrap fossils in damp paper and plaster to protect them. Each one is given a number.

Fossils are packed and taken away to be studied.

More to come

In 1965, paleontologists in Mongolia found the huge arms of a dinosaur called *Deinocheirus*. They are still looking for its body.

Deinocheirus's arms were longer than a man.

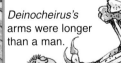

Dinosaur origins

It helps to understand why dinosaurs disappeared if you know where they came from. Most scientists think all living things gradually change. This change is called evolution.

Your environment is the area where you live. Evolution makes animals change, or evolve, to suit their environment.

Giraffes live in an environment with tall trees. They have evolved long necks to reach the leaves at the top.

From water to land

Here you can see how dinosaurs evolved over millions of years.

Over 350 million years ago, no animals lived on the land. But where pools began to dry up, some fish began to leave the water.

Eusthenopteron was a fish that used its strong fins like legs.

How to survive

Sometimes environments can change. Animals that are suited to the changes survive, but others die. A famous scientist, Charles Darwin, called this natural selection.

Not everybody believes in evolution and natural selection. Many people believe God created earth and put animals on it as they are now.

350 million years ago, animals with legs, called amphibians, evolved. They lived on land, but they had to be close to water to lay eggs.

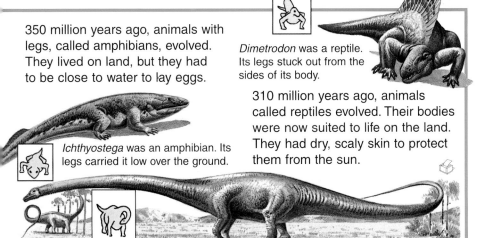

Dimetrodon was a reptile. Its legs stuck out from the sides of its body.

310 million years ago, animals called reptiles evolved. Their bodies were now suited to life on the land. They had dry, scaly skin to protect them from the sun.

Ichthyostega was an amphibian. Its legs carried it low over the ground.

Diplodocus had pillar-like legs.

230 million years ago, some reptiles evolved stronger and straighter legs. These were the first dinosaurs.

Natural selection at work

Peppered moths show how a changing environment can make animals evolve.

1. Some Peppered moths are dark and some are pale. 200 years ago there were more pale moths.

2. Pale moths were the same shade as trees, so birds caught more dark ones, which were easier to see.

3. When factories were built, smoke made the trees darker. Birds now found it easier to catch pale moths.

4. More dark moths survived and had dark babies. Dark moths soon became more common.

127

Shapes and sizes

Dinosaurs evolved into many different sizes. Some were quite small. Others were much bigger than any land animals alive today.

Brachiosaurus was one of the biggest dinosaurs. It could weigh more than 50 tonnes (51 tons). That's the same as nine elephants.

Brachiosaurus' back bones were light but very strong to help carry its heavy body.

Strong legs supported its weight.

Keeping warm

Animals cannot survive if they get too hot or too cold. A dinosaur's temperature changed with the heat of the sun. In cool weather, dinosaurs got cold.

The biggest dinosaurs were so huge that it took them a very long time to cool down. So their great size helped them to keep warm.

Using a sail

Spinosaurus had a special sail on its back to keep its body at the right temperature. As the sun moved, *Spinosaurus* changed position.

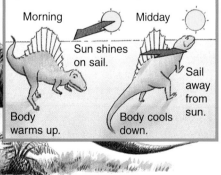

Morning
Sun shines on sail.
Body warms up.

Midday
Sail away from sun.
Body cools down.

Different shapes

Dinosaurs evolved into different shapes for different reasons.

Ceratopians had huge heads with bony frills and sharp horns. *Triceratops* was the biggest ceratopian. It was 11m (36ft) long and weighed 5.4 tonnes (6 tons).

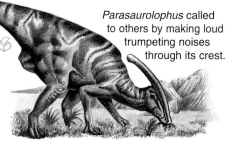

Parasaurolophus called to others by making loud trumpeting noises through its crest.

Parasaurolophus had a bony beak for tearing off plants to eat, and a bony crest on its head.

Triceratops had sharp horns to keep enemies away.

A bony frill protected its neck and held strong muscles for working its jaws.

Euoplocephalus was a heavy dinosaur covered in bony plates and spikes for protection.

Euoplocephalus used its tail as a club to defend itself.

Make a dinosaur

You could make a *Euoplocephalus* with balls of clay, used matches and thumbtacks.

Roll a big ball for the body.

Roll smaller balls for the head, legs and club.

Roll a sausage shape for the tail.

Use broken matches for the spikes.

For the bony plates, use thumbtacks.

129

Dinosaur life

Fossil clues help experts to find out how dinosaurs lived. This also helps them to discover what changes may have made dinosaurs die out.

Clues about food

Some dinosaurs had sharp teeth and strong claws. This shows that they ate meat. *Tyrannosaurus* was one of the biggest meat eaters. It was as heavy as an elephant and as long as a bus.

Tyrannosaurus had sharp teeth for cutting meat.

It had strong claws for tearing open its prey.

How you eat

People can eat many different kinds of food. You have different teeth for different jobs. Look at your mouth in a mirror and feel inside with clean fingers.

Can you feel sharp front teeth for cutting and flat back teeth for grinding?

Other dinosaurs had special teeth for eating plants. *Corythosaurus* was a plant eater. It chewed on tough leaves and twigs.

Corythosaurus's jawbone shows hundreds of small teeth for grinding plants.

Corythosaurus

Fossil dinosaur droppings can show what dinosaurs ate. Pine needles in dropping.

Eggs

Scientists know that some dinosaurs laid eggs, because they have found lots of fossil ones. The biggest eggs are over 30cm (1ft) across.

Baby *Protoceratops* hatched from eggs laid in the sand to keep them warm.

Staying together

Lots of fossil *Triceratops* have been found together. This shows that they probably lived in herds.

Experts think adult *Triceratops* surrounded their babies to protect them from danger.

Fossil footprints

Velociraptor was a fierce hunter. It was only 2m (6½ft) long, but its fossil footprints are spaced far apart. This shows how fast *Velociraptor* could run.

Velociraptor's long, stiff tail helped it to balance when it was running or jumping.

Long legs helped it to take big strides.

Fighting

Some dinosaurs that lived in herds fought each other to decide upon a leader. The thick skull bone of the male *Pachycephalosaurus* was probably used to protect it in fights.

Pachycephalosaurus fought with their heads, like goats do.

131

Alongside dinosaurs

While dinosaurs were living on the land, other prehistoric reptiles were living in the sea and the air. Interestingly, they disappeared at exactly the same time as dinosaurs.

Sea monsters

Huge reptiles lived in the sea. Their long, smooth bodies made them good swimmers. Their legs evolved into flippers to help them swim.

Ichthyosaurs grew up to 12m (38ft) long. They did not lay eggs, but gave birth to their young underwater.

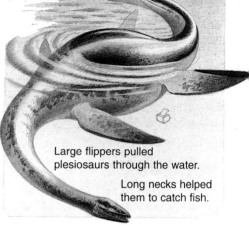

Large flippers pulled plesiosaurs through the water.

Long necks helped them to catch fish.

Plesiosaurs grew up to 12m (38ft) long. They came onto land to lay their eggs.

Ichthyosaurs could leap like dolphins.

Sharp teeth for catching fish

Big eyes for seeing underwater

Ichthyosaurs had hand bones inside their flippers. This shows they were reptiles and not fish.

In the air

Pterosaurs were flying reptiles. They had wings made of skin, just like bats today. They also had very light bones to help them fly. Some were no bigger than a sparrow. Others were the size of a small aircraft.

Pteranodon's wings were 6m (20ft) across. It lived on high cliffs.

Pterodactylus was a small pterosaur. It had sharp teeth for catching insects.

Pteranodon only weighed 17kg (37lbs), about the same as a five-year-old child.

First bird

Archaeopteryx was one of the first birds. It had feathers and it could fly like birds today. *Archaeopteryx* lived 150 million years ago. It was about the size of a crow.

Archaeopteryx's skeleton was very similar to those of small dinosaurs such as *Compsognathus*. This shows that birds probably evolved from dinosaurs.

Archaeopteryx had feathers for flying and keeping warm.

Compsognathus was a small dinosaur.

Archaeopteryx had a skeleton like a dinosaur's.

Claws for climbing trees

Internet link *For a link to a Web site where you can find out about the first birds, go to **www.usborne-quicklinks.com***

Why did they die?

Experts know when dinosaurs died out, but they are still not sure why. There are different ideas about what might have happened. Now scientists know many of these ideas are wrong.

Finding out from rocks

Fossil dinosaurs are found in rocks from the Mesozoic Era. But there are none in rocks that are newer than this.

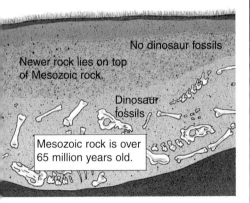

No dinosaur fossils

Newer rock lies on top of Mesozoic rock.

Dinosaur fossils

Mesozoic rock is over 65 million years old.

This shows that dinosaurs all became extinct 65 million years ago, at the end of the Mesozoic Era.

Too big?

Some scientists thought dinosaurs grew so huge that they could not support their own weight.

Now experts know that big dinosaurs had very strong skeletons.

Small dinosaurs became extinct too. So size cannot explain why they all died out.

Dying of diseases?

Some scientists thought diseases made dinosaurs extinct.

Some dinosaurs had diseases, but they evolved to survive these. Now experts know that disease on its own can never make a type of animal extinct.

Beaten by mammals?

During the Mesozoic Era, a new kind of creature called mammals evolved. (You can read more about them later.)

Some experts thought mammals ate all the dinosaurs' food.

Others thought mammals stole dinosaurs' eggs.

Now scientists are sure that mammals did not make dinosaurs extinct. Mammals only became important after dinosaurs died out.

Poisonous flowers?

The first flowering plants evolved during the Cretaceous Period. Some experts thought they had chemicals that poisoned dinosaurs.

Now scientists know that new kinds of dinosaurs evolved especially to eat the new plants.

End of the line

During the Mesozoic Era, new dinosaurs always evolved to take the place of others. But at the end of the Era, dinosaurs all died out together, and no more evolved to replace them.

Something must have happened that killed all the dinosaurs and stopped new ones from evolving. The next four pages tell you more about this.

DEAD END

Big changes

The environment changed in many different ways while dinosaurs lived on earth. Scientists think this might explain why dinosaurs died out.

Changes in plants

Many different kinds of plants evolved during the Mesozoic Era.

These plants lived during the Triassic and Jurassic Periods.

Cycads

Horsetails

These plants lived during the Cretaceous Period.

Flowering plants

Hardwood trees

Changes in plants meant dinosaurs' food was always changing too. But these changes were so gradual that dinosaurs could evolve to keep up.

Changes in the weather

The climate is the kind of weather that any place usually has.

Earth had a warm climate for most of the Mesozoic Era.

But at the end of the Cretaceous Period it became cooler. Experts think that cold weather helped to make dinosaurs extinct.

Most dinosaurs had no fur or feathers to help store their body heat. Most of them were too big to warm up again after a long, cold winter.

Changes in the earth's surface

The earth's surface is broken into large pieces called plates. These move around so that continents are always slowly changing position. This is called continental drift.

As the plates move, the earth's environment and climate change. Some experts think this made dinosaurs extinct. These maps show how the earth has changed.

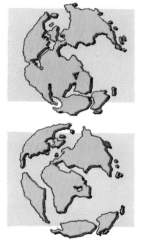

During the Triassic Period, there was just one big continent called Pangea. The climate was warm all around the world.

During the Cretaceous Period, Pangea split up into new continents and oceans were left in between them. Earth's climate became cooler.

This is what the earth looks like today. The continents are still moving, but it happens too slowly for you to tell.

In the sea

As the land changed, so did the sea. Some experts think this killed millions of tiny sea creatures called *Foraminifera*, and other animals that ate them.

Foraminifera and many other sea creatures died out with dinosaurs.

Too slow

Continental drift takes a very long time. On its own, it does not explain why dinosaurs and other creatures all died out so suddenly.

A sudden change

Now scientists think dinosaurs died out because something violent suddenly changed the earth's climate. Here is what may have happened.

Nothing left to eat

All living things in any environment depend upon each other for their food. This is called a food web.

Caterpillars eat leaves.

Shrews eat caterpillars.

Owls eat shrews.

If the dinosaurs' food web broke at the end of the Mesozoic Era, they would have died out. Here you can see why.

No plants

Plant eaters died.

Meat eaters died.

What broke the food web?

Many scientists think a big lump of rock from outer space, called an asteroid, struck the earth at the end of the Mesozoic Era.

The asteroid was probably 10 to 15km (6 to 9 miles) across.

Where it landed

There are clues that an asteroid hit what is now Yucatan in Mexico.

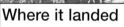

The asteroid landed here.

Mexico

Yucatan

Experts have found tiny glass beads like this around the area. They are made of rock that melted when the asteroid struck the earth.

No sunlight

All living things close to where the asteroid struck were killed. Dust and gases filled the air around the world. Sunlight was blocked out and the world became cold and dark.

Without sunlight, all the plants died.

When plants died, the food web broke down. This killed dinosaurs, and they soon became extinct.

How plants grow

You can see how plants need sunlight. Put some damp paper towels on a saucer and scatter cress seeds on it.

Leave the saucer in sunlight so the seeds can grow.

Cover some shoots.

Take the cover off after a week. The shoots without any sunlight will have died.

Volcanoes

65 million years ago there were also some huge volcanic eruptions in what is now India. These might have caused as much damage as an asteroid.

Some experts think dust and gases from these volcanoes might have blocked out the sunlight too.

Too hot?

When the asteroid struck, it threw up water droplets as well as dust. After the dust settled, water droplets stayed in the air. It trapped the heat of the sun, so the earth heated up like a giant greenhouse.

Just as dinosaurs would have been killed by cold, they also would have died if it was too hot.

After dinosaurs

Not everything became extinct at the end of the Mesozoic Era. Plants grew up from seeds that had survived, and soon other animals began to fill the places left by dinosaurs.

More birds evolved to live in the air.

Small mammals lived in the trees and forests.

Some reptiles, such as crocodiles and turtles, still lived in fresh water.

About mammals

Mammals are animals that can keep their bodies warm all the time. Most mammals have fur or hair and do not lay eggs. They give birth to babies and feed them on milk.

Purgatorius was the size of a rat. It ate insects, and came out at night when dinosaurs were asleep.

Purgatorius lived 70 million years ago when dinosaurs were still around. It probably slept during the day, and came out at night. All later mammals evolved from animals like this.

Staying alive

Mammals' warm bodies helped them to survive when the climate changed. They were also small enough to burrow holes and escape from the cold or heat.

Different kinds of mammal

The time since dinosaurs died out is called the Cenozoic Era. Many different mammals have evolved and died out during this time. Here you can see some that are now extinct.

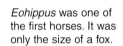

Saber-tooth cats were fierce hunters, just like tigers today.

Paraceratherium was the largest ever land mammal. It was 8m (26ft) tall, six times as high as a man.

Eohippus was one of the first horses. It was only the size of a fox.

Dinosaur relatives

Tuataras lived over 150 million years ago, at the same time as dinosaurs. Some still live in New Zealand today.

Tuatara

Chaffinch

Modern birds evolved from prehistoric birds like *Archaeopteryx*, and they still have very similar skeletons to dinosaurs. This shows that birds are dinosaurs' closest relatives today.

Out of the trees

People are mammals. Most experts think we evolved from creatures like apes that lived in the trees about 10 million years ago.

The first people were hunters who could walk upright on two legs. They learned how to use tools, build shelters and make fire.

141

Today

Since dinosaurs died out, many other living things have become extinct. Today most extinctions are caused by the things people do.

Damage to wildlife

Wildlife means all the wild plants and animals living in the world. The main danger to wildlife comes from people damaging or changing the environment where it lives.

On the island of Madagascar people have chopped down the forests where lemurs live. Now very few lemurs are left.

Pollution is waste, such as poisonous chemicals, left by people. Pollution in the environment harms everything that lives there.

Oil spilled in the sea kills many sea birds, such as cormorants.

Hunting

If animals are hunted too much, they can become extinct. People usually hunt animals for food or for their skins.

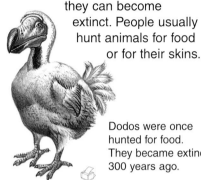

Dodos were once hunted for food. They became extinct 300 years ago.

Living together

It is important to protect wildlife. All living things are connected to each other by food webs. If one thing disappears, many others may suffer. For example, snakes eat rats. In parts of Africa, people killed lots of snakes. Soon there were too many rats. They ate people's crops, so people suffered.

Internet link For a link to a Web site that will tell you more about extinct animals and why they died out, go to **www.usborne-quicklinks.com**

Internet links

Go to **www.usborne-quicklinks.com** and type in the keywords "pocket scientist" for links to these Web sites about dinosaurs.

Web site 1 Take a virtual safari to find out about dinosaurs and why they disappeared.

Web site 2 Here you'll find answers to all your questions about dinosaurs and how they lived.

Web site 3 Find out how discoveries over the years have changed our view of dinosaurs.

Web site 4 Watch amazing animations of dinosaurs and see what their lives were like. You can also download a dinosaur screensaver for your computer.

Web site 5 Here you'll find information, games and quizzes about dinosaurs.

Web site 6 Join in an egg hunt and see how scientists "hatch" fossilized eggs.

Web site 7 Find out about dinosaur fossils and go on a virtual dig where you have to make the right choices to uncover the dinosaur bones.

Web site 8 Explore the history of dinosaur science, and take a look at a fascinating gallery of famous scientific mistakes.

Web site 9 Learn about the plants, insects and other animals that lived at the same time as the dinosaurs.

Web site 10 Find out how to make your own fossil prints.

For links to all these sites, go to www.usborne-quicklinks.com and type in the keywords "pocket scientist".

More Internet links

Here are some more Web sites you can visit to find out about dinosaurs. For links to all these sites, go to **www.usborne-quicklinks.com** and type in the keywords "pocket scientist".

Web site 1 Watch a movie all about dinosaurs and test your knowledge in a quiz.

Web site 2 Read the story of an amazing fossil discovery.

Web site 3 Find out more about dinosaurs and have fun with games and puzzles.

Web site 4 Here you can find useful facts and figures about all kinds of dinosaurs.

Web site 5 Learn how fossil scientists put together complete skeletons of dinosaurs, then test your fossil skills by matching dinosaur skeletons with their skulls.

Web site 6 Try a dinosaur quiz and find out about some fossilized dinosaur eggs found in Argentina.

Web site 7 E-mail the Dinosaur Man with your dinosaur questions.

Web site 8 Read more on the different theories about how dinosaurs became extinct.

Web site 9 Learn about the plants and animals that existed after the last dinosaurs died.

Web site 10 Sue is the largest and most complete *Tyrannosaurus rex* skeleton. Read about how scientists found her and put her bones together.

For links to all these sites, go to www.usborne-quicklinks.com and type in the keywords "pocket scientist".

HOW DOES A BIRD FLY?

Kate Woodward

Designed by Mary Forster
Illustrated by Isabel Bowring

Revised by Philippa Wingate
With thanks to Katarina Dragoslavić

Consultant: Robin Horner (Warden, RSPB)

CONTENTS

Early fliers

Some of the creatures that lived on earth over 200 million years ago, at the same time as the dinosaurs, could fly. They were called pterosaurs.

Pterosaur

Pterosaurs had wings made of leathery skin, not feathers. For this reason, scientists do not count them as birds.

Some pterosaurs had wings about 7m (almost 26ft) across. That's nearly as long as a bus.

Pterosaurs had jaws like beaks.

None of the dinosaurs could fly.

Compsognathus

The first bird

The first animal that scientists call a bird is the Archaeopteryx. It lived about 140 million years ago. They think it developed from dinosaurs that could not fly, not from the pterosaurs.

Archaeopteryx

It was about the size of a crow and had feathers on its body and wings.

Odd bird

This Hoatzin chick is similar to the earliest known birds. It has unusual claws on its wings, like an Archaeopteryx (see below). It lives in the forests of South America today.

The claws drop off the adult bird.

Fossil bird

Scientists have found the remains, or fossils, of Archaeopteryxes buried inside rock.

It had teeth and had claws on its wings to climb trees.

All kinds of birds

There are more than 8,650 kinds of birds in the world today and they are all very different. They live in places as cold as the North Pole and as hot as the tropical rainforests around the Equator.

Ostriches live on the grasslands in Africa. They cannot fly, but can run very fast.

Budgerigars are popular pets. Wild budgies live in large groups, or flocks, in Australia.

Geese live near water. Their young are called goslings.

Some penguins live in the Antarctic near the South Pole. They are very good swimmers, but cannot fly.

A bird's body

To help birds fly, their bodies are very streamlined. This means they are a smooth shape so they slip through the air easily. Here you can see the parts of a bird's body.

Feathers

Birds are the only animals with feathers. Small birds have about 1,000 feathers. Large birds can have as many as 25,000.

Eggs in a nest

All birds lay eggs. They do this so they do not have to carry their young around inside them before they are born.

Wings

Birds have wings instead of arms. They are strong and light enough to make a bird fly when it flaps them.

Feathers are made from keratin, like our hair.

Eyes

Many birds have eyes on opposite sides of their heads so they can see as much around them as possible.

Chicks

This beak is good for catching fish.

Beak

The shape of a bird's beak depends on what food it eats.

Neck

Birds have very bendable necks. They can turn their heads to point backward to clean themselves with their beaks.

Ears

A bird's ears are hard to see. But they can hear very quiet sounds.

Inside a bird

If a bird is too heavy it cannot fly. To make it lighter, its skeleton is made of hollow bones. These are full of air.

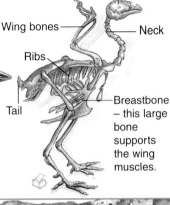

Skull

Wing bones

Neck

Ribs

Tail

Breastbone – this large bone supports the wing muscles.

Ear

Feet

Birds' feet vary in shape and size. Many use their toes to grip branches.

A kingfisher's feet are covered in scaly skin.

A lily trotter has very long toes to walk over soft mud.

A goose has webbed feet which it uses for paddling.

149

Feathers

Feathers keep birds warm, stop their bodies from getting wet and help them fly. All birds have different types of feathers. You can see them on this drake (male duck).

Down feathers

Down feathers are the very soft ones next to the bird's skin. They help keep the bird warm.

Tail feathers

Birds use their tail feathers to steer themselves in the air and to balance on the ground.

A woodpecker uses its tail to hold itself steady against a tree.

150

Wing feathers

The long feathers on the wings are the most important in helping the bird to fly.

The feathers on a bird's body are called its plumage.

Wing feathers

Tail feathers

Mallard

Body feathers

Body feathers

Body feathers lie smoothly over the down feathers. They are oily so that they are waterproof. This stops the bird from getting cold and wet.

Molting

Adult birds lose old feathers a few at a time and grow new ones. This is called molting.

Cleaning and preening

Birds spend a lot of time looking after their feathers to keep them clean and healthy. They pull each feather through the tip of their beak. This is called preening.

Scarlet macaw

Preening gets rid of tiny insects, such as lice, which like to live on feathers.

Feather color

Some birds have bright feathers so they get noticed. This helps to attract a mate. Lorikeet

Others have feathers the same color as the things around them, so they are hard to see and can hide from enemies.

Grouse

A flamingo has pink feathers. This color comes from the food it eats. Flamingo

Taking a bath

You can often see small birds bathing in water or in dust.

A bird gets dirt and lice off its feathers by rubbing itself in dust.

Making your own bird bath

Small birds like to splash in water. You can make a birdbath in your garden using an upturned old trashcan lid filled with water.

Borrow a bird book from your library to help you recognize birds that come to use it.

Internet link For a link to a Web site where you can see beautiful pictures of feathers under a microscope, go to **www.usborne-quicklinks.com**

Built to fly

Three types of animals can fly – birds, bats and insects. Birds are the best fliers because of the shape of their wings.

Not a bird

A bat is not a bird as it has no feathers. Its body is furry and it has leathery skin on its wings. It belongs to the type of animals called mammals.

Birdmen

In the past, men tried to fly like birds. They made wings and attached them to their arms, but were too heavy to fly.

The wing

A bird's wing is a special shape, rounded on top and curved underneath. This is called an airfoil and helps lift the bird as it flaps its wings.

In flight, air passes smoothly over the wing.

Airfoil shape

The long primary flight feathers are the main ones that power the bird through the air. Primary means "first".

The secondary flight feathers help make the airfoil shape.

Golden eagle

Wing coverts – The wing coverts help make the wing rounded on top.

In flight

A bird flaps its wings forward and down. The feathers are held together to push against the air. The bird flies forward.

The bird brings its wings upward and back to start another flap. As it does, the feathers twist open to let air through.

To change direction or go up and down, the bird tilts its body to one side and moves its wings or tail to steer through the air.

Make your own airfoil

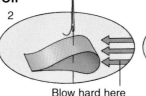

1

Glue here

Air on top presses less

3

Blow hard here

Air below pushes up

1. Bend a long piece of paper into an airfoil shape. Glue the ends together and a little way up the side edges as shown.

2. With an adult's help, thread string through the middle of the paper. Blow hard over the curved end of the paper. What happens?

3. Air rushes fast over the top of the airfoil. This air presses less against the airfoil than air below, so the airfoil rises.

Internet link For a link to a Web site that shows how a bird moves its wings to stay in the air, go to **www.usborne-quicklinks.com**

Different ways to fly

The shape of a bird's wing tells you something about how it flies. Next to the birds on these pages are small pictures of their wing shapes to help you to recognize them.

Speedy swallows

A swallow has curved, pointed wings. This good airfoil shape makes the air rush fast along the top of them. Swallows flap their wings very fast to speed along.

It tucks its short legs into its body while it is flying so they do not slow it down.

Swallows often rest on telephone wires.

154

Fastest bird

The peregrine falcon is a bird of prey. This means that it hunts other small birds and animals.

When it hunts, it circles high in the sky looking for prey.

Once it has spotted something, it dives at about 180kph (112mph) with its wings back. This is almost as fast as a race car. It is called stooping.

As it reaches its prey, the falcon swings its feet forward and knocks the victim with its claws.

Long distance fliers

Many geese, such as these snow geese, fly very long distances to where they nest. They fly for many hours without stopping and have long, broad wings which they do not need to flap very fast.

Geese often make a "honking" noise as they fly.

Straight from the nest

Once a chick is strong enough it flies from its nest. At first, it makes short, practice flights from bush to bush.

A mother tempts her chicks out of the nest with food.

Short flights

A jay has wide, blunt wings which it flaps slowly. This makes it easy to twist and turn through the trees.

Birds with wings this shape usually only fly for short distances.

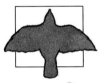

Internet link For a link to a Web site with photos of birds flying, go to **www.usborne-quicklinks.com**

155

Flying with the wind

Many birds use the wind to help them stay up in the air. Some keep their wings still and let the wind carry them along. Others beat their wings against the air to stay in one spot.

Riding on air

Many large birds stay in the air for a long time without flapping their wings. This is called gliding.

An albatross has very long, narrow wings for fast gliding over the sea.

An albatross hardly flaps its wings at all. It can fly like this for days just using the wind.

It spends most of its life out at sea and is rarely seen, except by sailors.

Gliding over the sea

Wind

1. The bird flies with the wind down toward the sea.

2. Flying fast, it turns toward the wind and rises up.

3. Then it turns and flies fast with the wind again.

High fliers

When the sun heats the ground, warm air spirals upward. These drafts of warm air are called thermals. Most large birds of prey use their long wings to soar upward on thermals.

Once it is at the top of a thermal it glides down to reach another.

Thermal

The bird is carried up high by the rising warm air. It does not need to flap its wings.

Vultures can soar for many hours at a time without becoming exhausted.

Staying in one spot

Many birds beat their wings fast against the air to stay in one spot. This is called hovering. A hummingbird hovers to feed.

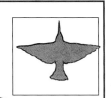

It beats its wings in a figure-eight shape almost 50 times every second.

Bird spotting

Try to recognize everyday birds by their wing shape. Draw them, then check in a guide to see what type they are.

Going up and coming down

Birds may live in trees, on water or on cliff tops so they take off and land in different ways. Most take off by springing into the air.

Running take-off

Large birds are too heavy to spring up. This coot has to run fast for a long way, splashing across the water, before it gets up in the air.

It stretches its neck out to make itself more streamlined.

Using sea breezes

Cormorants nest on cliff tops where there are strong sea breezes. They jump off cliffs with their wings open so the wind lifts them up.

Cormorants live in large groups called colonies.

Lazy flier

Pheasants do not like flying much. But if they are frightened they flap their broad wings and take off almost straight up in the air.

Their wings are short so they do not hit branches and trees.

Landing on a branch

All birds have to slow down before they can land safely.

As a bullfinch comes in to land it spreads its tail feathers out like a fan.

The feathers act like a brake and slow down the bird's flight.

It brings its feet forward, ready to land.

It flaps its wings back and forward to slow it down more.

Landing on water

A swan is one of the heaviest flying birds.

Swans land on water. They put their large webbed feet down first and push against the water. This slows them down before they land. They look as if they are water-skiing.

Its toes grip tight around the branch as it lands, so it does not fall off.

As it settles, the bird closes its tail feathers and tucks in its wings.

Migration

Many kinds of birds fly from one part of the world to another every year. This is called migration. They make this long journey to a warmer place where there is plenty of food.

Birds on the moon
In the past people did not know where birds spent the winter. Some thought that they flew to the moon.

Following stars
Birds find their way by watching the sun during the day and following the stars at night. Something inside them acts like a clock. It tells them when to set off.

Bad weather
During bad weather, when the sun is hidden by clouds, birds can lose their way.

Before the journey
Before they set off, birds eat plenty of food to store up energy for their journey.

BRITISH ISLES

EUROPE

ATLANTIC OCEAN

SAHARA DESERT

BRAZIL

SOUTH AMERICA

The shearwater's journey takes fewer than 20 days.

Over oceans
Manx shearwaters migrate across the Atlantic Ocean to the coast of Brazil. They return to northern Europe once the weather is warmer there.

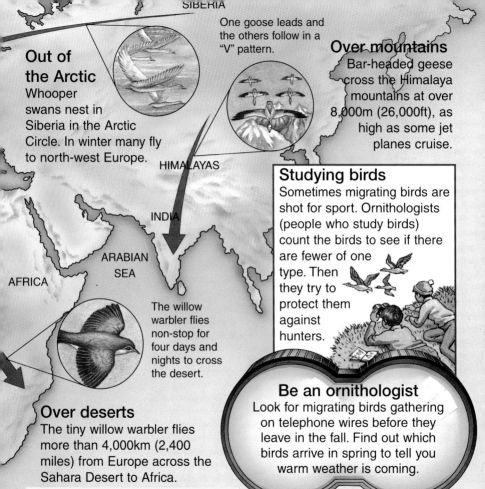

SIBERIA

Out of the Arctic

Whooper swans nest in Siberia in the Arctic Circle. In winter many fly to north-west Europe.

One goose leads and the others follow in a "V" pattern.

Over mountains

Bar-headed geese cross the Himalaya mountains at over 8,000m (26,000ft), as high as some jet planes cruise.

HIMALAYAS

INDIA

ARABIAN SEA

AFRICA

The willow warbler flies non-stop for four days and nights to cross the desert.

Studying birds

Sometimes migrating birds are shot for sport. Ornithologists (people who study birds) count the birds to see if there are fewer of one type. Then they try to protect them against hunters.

Over deserts

The tiny willow warbler flies more than 4,000km (2,400 miles) from Europe across the Sahara Desert to Africa.

Be an ornithologist

Look for migrating birds gathering on telephone wires before they leave in the fall. Find out which birds arrive in spring to tell you warm weather is coming.

Internet link For a link to a bird sanctuary Web site, go to **www.usborne-quicklinks.com**

Night owls

Most owls do not fly around much during the day. This is because they are roosting, or sleeping. They come out at night to hunt.

Night hunters

Owls are good at hunting at night. Their wings, eyes and ears are specially made to make flying and hunting in the dark easier.

A tawny owl has shorter wings than some other owls, for flying among trees.

Owls have huge eyes. Some are almost as big as human eyes.

Their ears are behind the face feathers, called the facial disc, at the side of their head.

Owls have sharp, hooked beaks for carrying and tearing up their food.

These sharp claws, called talons, are for catching and killing food.

Tawny owl

Facial disc

Soft fringe

An owl has soft fringe on the edge of its wing feathers. These help it fly almost silently, so that small animals do not hear it coming.

Protecting our owls

Some owls lose their homes and hunting grounds when farmers cut down trees to make new fields. You can find out which owls are threatened and how to help by joining a local bird club. Your library will help you find one.

Hunting for food

A barn owl is an agile flier. It has large, broad wings which it flaps slowly. It can take off vertically, stop suddenly in mid-flight and hover in one spot. It needs to do all these to hunt well.

When he hears a mouse, he flies overhead and hovers for a moment. Then he pounces.

Barn owl

The owl glides silently through the air listening for sounds and watching the ground.

Waiting for supper

Before they can fly, the young owls wait at the nest for their parents to bring food.

At the last moment, he swings his sharp talons forward to catch the mouse.

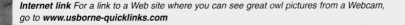

Internet link For a link to a Web site where you can see great owl pictures from a Webcam, go to **www.usborne-quicklinks.com**

Birds that can't fly

There are a few birds that can't fly. Some have found different ways to get around, such as swimming or running, so they no longer need to fly.

Champion swimmers

Penguins can't fly because their wings have become more like flippers. They use them to swim.

Their flippers are short and thin, like paddles. Penguins use them to push themselves along underwater.

Birds of the past
The giant elephant bird once lived on Madagascar and the dodo on Mauritius, both islands off Africa.

Elephant bird

Madagascar

Mauritius

Penguins have a very thick layer of tightly-packed feathers covering their bodies to keep them warm in the frozen Antarctic.

Emperor penguin

They swim near the surface of the water and dive down to catch fish.

When people went to live there, they hunted the birds and stole their eggs. Soon there were no birds left.

They could not fly to safety as they had such tiny wings.

Dodo

Flightless cormorants

Cormorants living on the Galapagos Islands have no enemies. They have lost the ability to fly because they do not need to.

They have plenty of food to eat from the seas around the islands.

Adélie penguins often march one after the other "following the leader" across the snow.

Adélie penguin

They waddle as they walk, using their flippers to balance.

Too heavy to fly

An ostrich is about 2.5m (8ft) tall and weighs 150kg (330lbs), almost as much as two people. It is too heavy to fly, but runs very fast.

Birds which weigh more than 15-20kg (30-45lbs) are too heavy to fly.

Amazing fliers

On this page you can find out about some amazing flying feats.

Non-stop flier

Swifts can fly for up to three years non-stop. They eat, drink, bathe and sleep as they fly.

One swift lived for 16 years and could have flown up to eight million km (nearly five million miles). This equals 200 times around the world.

Biggest flying bird

The Andean condor is the biggest flying bird in the world. Its wings spread out from tip to tip are 3.2m (nearly 11ft). It uses them to glide in thermal currents.

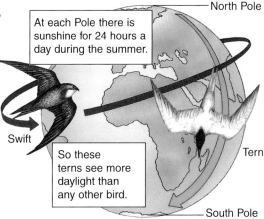

The greatest traveler

The Arctic tern makes the longest migration of all birds. Each year it flies from the Arctic Circle to the Antarctic and back again, to spend the summer at each Pole.

North Pole

At each Pole there is sunshine for 24 hours a day during the summer.

Swift

So these terns see more daylight than any other bird.

Tern

South Pole

Its wings are nearly four times the length of your arms outstretched.

Smallest bird

The bee hummingbird from Cuba is the smallest bird in the world. It is only 57mm (2¼ inches) from beak to tail. This is about as long as your thumb.

The hummingbird gets its name from the noise its wings make as it hovers.

Internet links

Go to **www.usborne-quicklinks.com** and type in the keywords "pocket scientist" for links to these Web sites about birds.

Web site 1 Here you'll find a gallery of fantastic photographs of birds.

Web site 2 Useful information and some fun activities, including a great pop-up card to make.

Web site 3 An online bird magazine with discussion groups, poetry and lots of information.

Web site 4 See illustrations of many different kinds of birds and find out about the latest sightings of rare birds.

Web site 5 Find out what people are doing to protect animals in danger, and how you can help.

Web site 6 Fascinating facts, including information about the rarest, the most common and the largest birds.

Web site 7 Find out how you can get involved in bird-watching and protecting endangered species on this Web site for enthusiasts.

Web site 8 Look at amazing pictures of nesting birds from a Nest Box Cam.

Web site 9 Lots of bird-themed jokes to chuckle over, or groan at!

Web site 10 See amazing photographs and video clips of bald eagles taken by a Webcam. You can hear sound clips too.

For links to all these sites, go to www.usborne-quicklinks.com and type in the keywords "pocket scientist".

More Internet links

Here are some more Web sites to visit to find out about birds. For links to all these sites, go to **www.usborne-quicklinks.com** and type in the keywords "pocket scientist".

Web site 1 Look at fantastic photographs of birds.

Web site 2 Click on an area of the world map for links to Web sites with photographs and information on birds from that region.

Web site 3 Here you can see great photographs of many different kinds of rare birds.

Web site 4 Watch a sequence of amazing pictures that chart the growth of two baby peregrine falcons, from hatching to getting ready to fly.

Web site 5 Facts about all kinds of birds, with detailed drawings.

Web site 6 Learn about migration by following the story of Max, an American golden plover, and his first journey south. You can read about the different places he passes through on his journey.

Web site 7 Take a tour of a virtual penguin museum.

Web site 8 Here you'll find lots of interesting facts about hummingbirds and swifts.

Web site 9 Find out all about bird-watching and get tips on how to go about identifying birds from their size, shape, sound and distinctive characteristics.

For links to all these sites, go to www.usborne-quicklinks.com and type in the keywords "pocket scientist ".

WHY DO TIGERS HAVE STRIPES?

Mike Unwin

Designed by Sharon Bennet

Illustrated by Robert Morton, Steven Kirk, Gillian Miller,
Robert Gillmor, Treve Tamblin and Stuart Trotter

Edited by Helen Edom and revised by Philippa Wingate
With thanks to Non Figg and Katarina Dragoslavić

Consultant: Dr. Margaret Rostron

CONTENTS

A world of colors

Many animals, such as tigers, have interesting colors or patterns. This section explains how colors and patterns help all kinds of animals from the fiercest tigers to the most helpless insects.

A tiger has a striped pattern. Can you think of any other animals with stripes?

Matching colors

Different animals' colors often match the places where they live. The oryx is an antelope that lives in the desert. Its pale color matches the sandy background.

In deserts there are few places to hide from enemies. Sandy animals are hard to spot because they blend in. Colors or patterns that help animals to hide are called camouflage.

Some desert animals live in holes. When they come out their sandy-colored camouflage helps them hide from hunters such as hawks and foxes.

An oryx is pale like the desert.

Scorpion

Gerbil

Hidden hunters

Most animals run away if they see a hunter coming. Camouflage helps hunters to hide so they can catch other animals to eat.

Snowy owls live in the Arctic where there is lots of snow. They hunt small creatures called lemmings. The owls' white feathers match the snow. It is hard for lemmings to spot them.

Lemmings

White feathers blend in with the snow and sky.

Forest greens

Many animals that live in rainforests are green to match the colors of the leaves. This camouflage makes them very hard to see.

Look at the green tree frog in this picture. How many other animals can you spot?

Tree frog

Blue waters

Camouflage is also important under the sea. Many sharks and other fish are blue or grey to blend in with the colors underwater.

Blue sharks

Internet link For a link to a Web site with shark videos, go to **www.usborne-quicklinks.com**

171

Patterns

Background colors are not the only kind of camouflage. Patterns also help animals to hide.

Breaking up shapes

A tiger in the zoo looks big, bright and easy to see. But in the forests and long grass where it hunts, a tiger can be hard to see. A tiger's stripes seem to break up its shape into small pieces. It is hard to see among the patterns and shadows of the background. This helps it to creep up on animals.

Seeing in black and white

This black and white picture shows how a leopard looks to an antelope.

Many animals, such as antelope, cannot see colors. They see in black and white. This makes it very hard for them to make out an animal, such as a leopard, whose pattern breaks up its shape.

Lying in wait

The gaboon viper is a snake that lives on the ground in African forests. Its complicated pattern makes its shape hard to see against the leaves.

Small animals cannot see a gaboon viper lying in wait for them. When they get close, the viper kills them with a bite from its poisonous fangs.

From a distance

The ringed plover lives on beaches. Close up its markings look bright. But from a distance you can only see a pattern that looks like the pebbles.

If the plover keeps still, it seems to disappear into the stony background. Enemies cannot spot it unless they are close.

Ringed plover

Seaweed shapes

The sargassum fish has strange lumps of skin that stick out from its body. These make its shape hard to see. It seems to disappear among the seaweed where it lives.

People hiding

Soldiers wear uniforms with special patterns. This helps them to blend into the background, just like tigers do.

Internet link For a link to a Web site which shows how animals blend in with their surroundings, go to **www.usborne-quicklinks.com**

173

Shadows and light

Light and shadows can make animals stand out from their background.

Lying flat

This bird is called a stone curlew. It is well camouflaged but you can still see its shadow. In the daylight, solid things always have shadows. This helps you to see where they are.

Shadow disappears

A stone curlew lies flat on the ground so it looks small. This makes its shadow disappear so it is even harder for enemies to spot.

Stone curlew's shadow

Flat shapes

Some animals have flattened bodies. Enemies do not notice them because they leave hardly any shadow.

Flaps of skin on a gecko's tail make it look flat.

The flying gecko is a lizard that lives on tree trunks. It has a flat body with flaps of skin that press down on the bark. This helps it to hide.

174

Dark and pale

You can often spot solid things by seeing the light shining on them.

Sunlight makes the top of this rock look lighter than the background.

No sunlight reaches the bottom, so it looks darker than the background.

The impala, like many animals, is colored dark above and pale below. This is the opposite of the natural light and shadow that fall on its body. It makes the impala harder to pick out from its background.

From below

Many water birds, such as puffins, are white underneath. They swim on the surface of the water and dive down to catch fish.

From underwater the surface looks bright because of sunlight above it. It is hard for fish to spot puffins from below. Their white undersides are hidden against the bright surface of the water.

Hiding with mirrors

Many sea fish, such as shad, have shiny silver scales on their sides and bellies. Underwater, these scales work like mirrors. They reflect the color of the water, so the fish become almost invisible.

175

Disguises

Some animals are shaped to look like other things. This helps them to hide. These insects all have disguises that help them hide in forests.

This caterpillar looks just like a bird dropping, so nothing wants to eat it.

The thorn bug looks just like a thorn on a branch.

The leaf butterfly's folded wings look like a leaf on the forest floor.

The stick insect looks just like twigs.

Standing straight

Animals can help their disguises to work by the way they behave. The tawny frogmouth is a bird with colors like bark. If it is in danger, it points its beak upward so it looks like a dead branch.

Deadly flowers

The flower mantis is a hunting insect. Its body is the same color and shape as the flowers where it hides.

Other insects that visit the flower do not notice the mantis lying in wait to catch them.

Like a log

A crocodile in the water can look just like a floating log. This disguise helps it to catch antelope that come to the water to drink.

The crocodile's rough skin looks like old tree bark.

Dressing up

Some animals disguise themselves by decorating their bodies. The sponge crab lives on the sea bed. It holds a sponge on its back legs.

This helps the crab to look like part of the sea bed.

Antelope don't notice the crocodile. When it gets close, it grabs an antelope with its huge jaws and pulls it into the water.

Internet link For a link to a Web site about crocodiles, go to **www.usborne-quicklinks.com**

Surprises

Some animals stop enemies attacking by tricking or surprising them. They often use colors or patterns to help.

Frightening eyes

Many hunters are frightened if they suddenly see a big pair of eyes.

This swallowtail caterpillar has patterns that look like eyes. Birds think they belong to a bigger, more dangerous creature, so they leave the caterpillar alone.

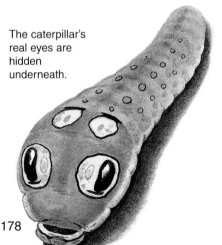

The caterpillar's real eyes are hidden underneath.

A bright flash

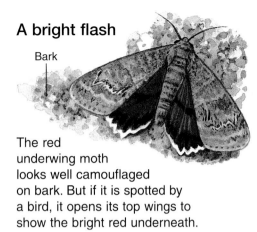

Bark

The red underwing moth looks well camouflaged on bark. But if it is spotted by a bird, it opens its top wings to show the bright red underneath.

A sudden flash of red surprises the bird. It leaves the moth alone.

Missing the target

This hairstreak butterfly has a pattern on its wings that looks like another head. Birds peck at the wings by mistake. This gives the butterfly time to escape.

Head pattern

The real head is at this end.

Puffing up

Some animals make themselves look bigger to trick enemies. A long-eared owl spreads its wings and puffs up its feathers to frighten enemies away.

This owl looks twice as big as usual.

Playing dead

Some hunters, such as hawks, only attack living creatures. An opossum is a small animal that pretends to be dead when it is in danger. When the danger has gone, the opossum gets up again.

An opossum pretends to be dead by rolling over with its mouth open.

Looking both ways

In India, tigers sometimes attack farmers. Tigers are scared by people's faces so they attack from behind. Farmers wear masks on the backs of their heads to scare tigers away.

Keep-away colors

Some animals do not try to hide. They have bright colors and patterns that are meant to be seen. These colors are a warning to their enemies.

Remembering colors

Black and yellow patterns are easy for animals to remember. Wasps are bright yellow and black. They can give their enemies a painful sting.

Black and yellow are warning colors.

If a young bird is stung by a wasp, it remembers its pattern. It will not try to catch a wasp again, because it knows that black and yellow things hurt.

Eating bees

A few birds, such as bee-eaters, have found a way to eat bees safely. They are not put off by warning colors. Bee-eaters strike a bee against a branch so its sting is squeezed out and broken.

Being seen

Many poisonous animals do not run away. Instead they show off their warning colors to their enemies.

The deadly poisonous arrow-poison frog does not hop away from enemies like other frogs do. It crawls around slowly so it can easily be seen.

Fierce black and white

The ratel is an African badger. Its white back makes it easy to see. Although it is quite small, it is very fierce and is not afraid of any other animal.

The ratel has strong teeth and claws.

The ratel does not need to keep a look-out for danger like most animals do. Its colors warn enemies that it is too dangerous to attack.

Smelly warning

Skunks are small animals with a bold pattern. They can squirt a nasty, smelly liquid at enemies such as dogs.

A spotted skunk stands up on its front legs to show its pattern. This warns the dog to stay back. If the dog comes closer, the skunk sprays it.

Signals for people

People use warning color just like animals do. Red often means "hot", "stop" or "danger".

This red tap warns you to be careful because the water is hot.

181

Copying colors

Some animals survive because they have colors and patterns that help them to look like other kinds of animals.

Poisonous or safe

Can you tell the difference between these two snakes? The coral snake is very poisonous. Its bright colors are a warning.

The king snake looks like a coral snake, but it is not poisonous at all. If you look hard you can see its pattern is slightly different.

King snake

Other animals are afraid to attack the king snake because it looks like a poisonous coral snake.

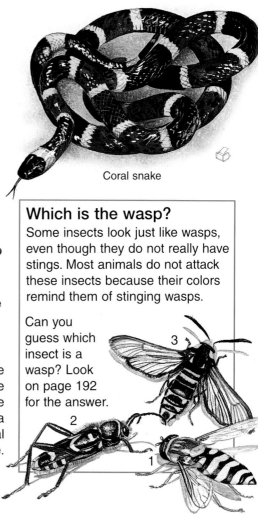

Coral snake

Which is the wasp?

Some insects look just like wasps, even though they do not really have stings. Most animals do not attack these insects because their colors remind them of stinging wasps.

Can you guess which insect is a wasp? Look on page 192 for the answer.

3

2

1

Ant antics

Most animals leave ants alone because they bite and sting. Some kinds of spiders look and behave like ants to fool their enemies.

Ants

The spider holds up two of its eight legs so it appears to have only six legs, like an ant.

The spider's upright front legs look like an ant's feelers.

Getting closer

The cleaner fish helps bigger fish by cleaning unwanted dirt and lice from their skin.

Cleaner fish

The saber-tooth blenny looks like a cleaner fish, but it is really a hunter that tricks other fish.

Saber-tooth blenny

Big fish let the blenny come near because they think it is a cleaner fish. But the blenny attacks them and takes bites out of their fins.

Whose egg?

Can you tell which of these eggs does not belong?

Reed warbler

The middle one is a cuckoo's egg. The rest belong to the reed warbler.

The cuckoo lays its egg in a reed warbler's nest. It is the same color as the eggs that are already there. The warblers think the cuckoo's egg is their own so they look after it.

Signals

Some kinds of animals use colors and patterns as signals to each other.

Danger

A rabbit has a short, fluffy white tail. If it sees an enemy such as a fox, it runs quickly back to its burrow, flashing its tail in the air.

The white tail is a signal to other rabbits. It says "danger!".

Follow my leader

Ring-tailed lemurs are animals with long black and white tails. When a group of lemurs is on the move, they hold their tails up like flags.

Lemurs' tails help them to see each other and stay together. They are signals that say "follow me".

Getting angry

A tiger has bold, white spots on its ears. If one tiger is angry with another, it turns the backs of its ears forward to show the white spots.

The white spots are a signal that warns other tigers to keep away.

Internet link For a link to a Web site with lots of information about how tigers live and hunt, go to **www.usborne-quicklinks.com**

Looking different

Colors can make it easier to tell similar animals apart. This helps animals to recognize others of their own kind.

Goldfinch

Chaffinch

These are the wings of two different finches. Their shape and size are the same, but the patterns and colors help to tell them apart.

People's colors

People also use colors to tell each other apart. All sports teams wear their own colors. This stops them getting mixed up with each other.

Different soccer teams wear different colors.

Being fed

Baby birds in nests wait for their parents to bring food. The babies' mouths are brightly colored inside.

These baby great tits have bright orange mouths.

When a parent arrives with food, the babies open their mouths wide to show the color inside. This is a signal to the parent. It says "feed me!".

Mysterious lights

Hatchet fish live deep at the bottom of the sea, where it is very dark. They have small patches on their bodies that light up and flash on and off.

Scientists think these lights could be signals to help hatchet fish recognize each other.

185

Showing off

Many male animals have bright colors to make them look attractive to females. This helps to bring the male and female together to breed.

Bright or brown

Male and female birds often look different from each other.

A male golden pheasant has beautifully colored feathers which he shows off to attract a female.

The female pheasant has much duller colors. This helps her to hide when she is protecting her eggs and chicks.

Risky colors

Bright colors can also attract enemies. In spring, a male paradise whydah's bright colors are easy to spot, and his long tail makes it hard for him to fly away.

After the whydah has found a female he loses his colors and long tail. For the rest of the year he stays plain brown.

Putting on a show

Some male birds put on a show to attract females. Every spring, male ruffs gather together. They puff up their feathers and fight. Females choose the males that put on the best show.

Three different male ruffs fighting

Colorful lizards

A male anolis lizard has an orange flap of skin under his throat. Usually it is folded up. But sometimes the lizard puffs it out and nods his head to show off the color.

The bright throat attracts females. It also warns other males to keep out of the area.

Fierce faces

Mandrills are African monkeys. A male mandrill has a colorful face that gets brighter when he is looking for a female. The biggest and fiercest males are brightest of all.

A female mandrill chooses the male with the brightest colors. Other males keep away from him.

Collecting colors

A male bowerbird attracts a female by building a pile of twigs called a bower. He then decorates it with shells, flowers and bright, shiny things.

A female bowerbird chooses the male with the best bower. She then builds a nest and lays the eggs.

Making colors

Fur, feathers, scales and skins can be all sorts of colors. Animals get these colors in many different ways.

Colors from food

Flamingos' feathers are pink because of a coloring called carotene which is found on water plants. Flamingos get carotene by eating tiny water animals that feed on these plants.

Often flamingos in zoos are not as pink as wild ones, because there is not enough carotene in their food.

Shiny colors

Many birds, such as sunbirds, have bright, shiny feathers. These change color when light falls on them from different directions.

This sunbird's feathers change from blue to green as the light shines on them.

Killed for colors

Some snakes are becoming rarer because people kill them for their beautiful skins.

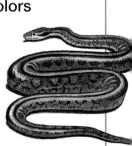

This bag is made from the skin of a python.

Growing green

Animals do not normally grow green fur. But this sloth looks green. This is because tiny green plants called algae grow in its fur.

Jigsaw

Butterflies' patterns are made by thousands of tiny different-colored scales that fit together.

Peacock butterfly scales

This is how the wing of a peacock butterfly looks close up. Can you see how the scales are arranged in rows?

Black fur

Animals have a kind of coloring in their bodies called melanin. Melanin makes dark colours in fur and skin.

A black panther is really a leopard born with more melanin than usual. Its fur is black. But if you look closely you can still see the spots.

White all over

Some animals are born white. They have no melanin so they cannot make dark colors. These are called albino animals.

An albino blackbird has white feathers.

Internet link For a link to a Web site where you can tour a butterfly house, go to **www.usborne-quicklinks.com**

189

Changes

Some animals can change their colors. Chameleons are lizards that change the color of their skin to match different backgrounds.

This chameleon has a green pattern when it is hiding among leaves.

On sandy ground the same chameleon turns brown. It is always very hard to spot.

Sole survivor

The sole is a flatfish. It hides from enemies by lying flat on the sea bed. Its color depends on where it lies.

This sole is the color and pattern of the pebbles on which it is lying. If it moves onto mud, it becomes a muddy color.

Sudden changes

If an octopus is in danger, different colors flash over its body. This surprises enemies and gives the octopus time to escape.

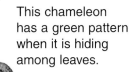

Colors also show how an octopus feels. For example, an angry octopus often turns red.

190

Internet links

Go to **www.usborne-quicklinks.com** and type in the keywords "pocket scientist" for links to these Web sites about animals and camouflage.

Web site 1 Here you can find out more about wildlife and issues that affect our planet. There are fact sheets on endangered species, including rhinoceroses, tigers, giant pandas and whales.

Web site 2 Lots of facts and information about different types of mammals.

Web site 3 Free pictures of animals to copy onto your computer and print out.

Web site 4 Imagine that you are a zoo keeper preparing to look after a six-year-old Siberian tiger. You need to build it a home and choose the right food to make sure it thrives in your zoo.

Web site 5 Here you'll find links to Webcams in wildlife parks all over Africa. This fabulous site also includes images of some of the recent highlights from them.

Web site 6 Lots of information about different types of habitats, including tropical rainforests, polar and mountainous regions and woodland areas, and profiles of some of the animals that live in them. You can also play the bobcat simulation game to see how well you would survive as a female bobcat.

For links to all these sites, go to www.usborne-quicklinks.com and type in the keywords "pocket scientist".

More Internet links

Here are some more Web sites to visit to find out about animals and camouflage. For links to all these sites, go to **www.usborne-quicklinks.com** and type in the keywords "pocket scientist".

Web site 1 Find out about animals which can change their color and why they might do it.

Web site 2 Find out how desert animals survive in hot, dry conditions, and how they make use of the little water available.

Web site 3 Learn all about the animals of the Arctic and how they survive in the ice and snow.

Web site 4 Find out wildlife news and read about how you can help to protect animals.

Web site 5 Here you'll find wildlife facts and pictures, plus games, jokes and quizzes.

Web site 6 View animals photographed in infrared light and see the difference between warm-blooded and cold-blooded animals.

Web site 7 Explore animal homes such as caves, trees and nests.

Web site 8 Play a game where you look for the camouflaged animals.

Web site 9 Find out about some of the amazing and disgusting ways that animals protect themselves.

Insect answers
Page 182 None of the insects in the picture is really a wasp. Number 1 is a fly, number 2 is a beetle and number 3 is a moth. You can see a real wasp on page 180.

For links to all these sites, go to www.usborne-quicklinks.com and type in the keywords "pocket scientist".

WHAT MAKES A FLOWER GROW?

Susan Mayes

Designed by Mike Pringle
Illustrated by Brin Edwards and Mike Pringle

Revised by Philippa Wingate
With thanks to Katarina Dragoslavić and Rosie Dickins

Series editor: Heather Amery

CONTENTS

All about flowers

Thousands of different flowers grow all over the world. They grow in gardens, on vegetables, on trees, in streets, in hedges and in your home.

Flowers are all kinds of colors, shapes and sizes. Some of them have very strong smells.

194

Insects and other tiny animals visit them. Most flowers die each year and grow again later.

Some flowers live in very hot countries and others live in cold places. Very strange flowers grow in some parts of the world.

Why do flowers have different colors and smells? Why do they grow again and what do they need to grow well?

What are the strangest flowers? You can find out about all of these things in this section.

195

Taking a close look

If you look closely at a flower, you can see that it has different parts. Each part has a special job.

Looking at a poppy

A baby flower, called a bud, grows safely inside two sepals.

Sepal

Bud

Sepals protect the bud and stop birds and insects from eating it.

Petal

As the bud grows, it opens up and the petals stretch out.

The stigma is sticky. It grows on top of the pistil.

The pistil is in the middle of the flower. New seeds will grow inside. It is sometimes called the seed box.

Pistil

Stigma

Stamen

The stamens grow around the pistil.

On top of each stamen there are tiny specks of golden dust, called pollen.

Internet link For a link to a Web site where you can find more information about the different parts of a flower, go to **www.usborne-quicklinks.com**

Different flowers

Most flowers have the same main parts, but they are all kinds of different colors, shapes and sizes.

A yellow water lily has big sepals around the outside and lots of short petals in the middle.

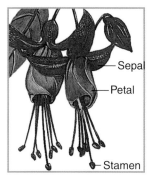

Fuchsias have long stamens and colorful sepals and petals.

A daffodil has one long stigma which grows from the pistil.

The petals of the snapdragon are all joined together.

197

Who visits a flower?

Flowers all over the world are visited by small animals, birds and many kinds of insects.

Tiny birds

A hummingbird hovers in front of brightly colored flowers to drink the nectar with its long beak.

Bats

In some countries, bats fly to flowers which open in the evening. They search for nectar and pollen.

Most animals go to flowers to look for pollen and sweet liquid food inside, called nectar.

Honey bees visit all kinds of flowers, looking for food to store for the winter.

Butterflies settle on buddleia flowers to drink nectar with their long tongues.

A bumble bee crawls into a foxglove to find the sweet food.

Flower signals

Many flowers use special signals which make the insects and tiny creatures come to visit them.

Colors

Special colors and markings guide bees to flowers and show them where to find the pollen inside.

You cannot see some markings but bees can. They do not see colors and shapes the same way as we do.

Smells

Most flowers have a sweet smell. It comes from the petals and tells visitors there is food nearby.

Honeysuckle has a strong smell at night. This is when the moths come out to find nectar for food.

A nasty smell

Flies visit a stapelia flower to lay their eggs. They come because it looks and smells like rotting meat.

Internet link For a link to a Web site where you can try an experiment to find out what color flowers bees prefer, go to **www.usborne-quicklinks.com**

Visitors at work

Insects and other small animals help plants when visiting them for food. They carry pollen from flower to flower. This will make seeds grow.

When a bee lands on a flower, some pollen from the stamens rubs off on to its body.

The bee flies to the next flower and some pollen rubs off on to the flower's stigma.

More pollen sticks to the bee as it crawls around on each flower it visits.

Open or closed

Flowers are not open to visitors if the weather is bad. They close to keep the pollen dry and safe.

A day-time flower closes up its petals at night to stop the dew from wetting the pollen inside.

Pollen in the air

Some plants' pollen is carried from plant to plant by the wind.

Tiny grains

Some trees have flowers called catkins. Their tiny, golden grains of pollen blow away in the wind.

Grass has flowers at the top of the stalk. The pollen is high up so it blows away easily.

Pollen clouds

In the summer, you can sometimes see clouds of pollen in the air. People who suffer from hay fever sneeze and sneeze.

Did you know?

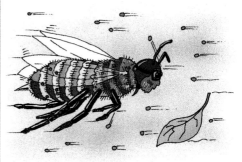

Pollen grains carried by flower visitors are sticky, but pollen grains in the air are smooth and dry.

Internet link For a link to a Web site where you can find out more about pollination, go to **www.usborne-quicklinks.com**

All about seeds

A plant cannot grow seeds until pollen reaches its stigma. And the pollen must be from the same kind of plant.

Pollen

Stigma

Stigma

Eggs

Seed box

1. Grains of pollen, carried by visitors, or blown by the wind, land on a new flower. They stick to the stigma.

2. The grains travel down into the tiny eggs inside the seed box. They make the eggs grow into seeds.

Stamen

3. The flower doesn't need its petals and stamens any more, so they drop off. Only the seed box is left.

4. The seeds grow inside until they are ripe. The seeds of this plant leave through small holes.

202

Kinds of seeds

Many different plants have seeds which you can eat.

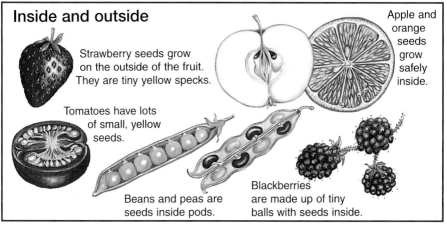

Sweet chestnuts, walnuts and coconuts are three kinds of seeds which come from trees.

Sunflower seeds are used to make oil and margarine. You can also eat them from the flower.

Inside and outside

Strawberry seeds grow on the outside of the fruit. They are tiny yellow specks.

Apple and orange seeds grow safely inside.

Tomatoes have lots of small, yellow seeds.

Beans and peas are seeds inside pods.

Blackberries are made up of tiny balls with seeds inside.

Seeds on the move

Popping out

The seeds of an iris grow inside colorful, round fruit. When the fruit is ripe, the seeds leave by popping out on to the ground.

Old Man's Beard

This is the name for the big, fluffy balls from a clematis plant. They are carried by the wind, with the seeds inside.

Seeds leave plants in different ways. Most of them are blown in the wind or are carried by animals.

Birds like to eat brightly colored seeds. They carry them away.

Seeds with hooks or sticky hairs, stick to birds and animals.

Conkers are the seeds of horse chestnut trees. They fall to the ground in green, spiky cases.

Seeds from a sycamore tree spin to the ground like helicopters.

Dandelion seeds blow away in the wind.

When poppy seeds are ripe, they pop out of the pod.

Ants carry some seeds away and store them for winter food.

Many of the seeds will die or be eaten, but some are covered by soil or leaves. They stay there all winter until spring comes.

Rolling along

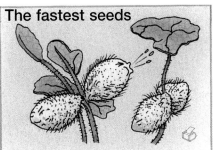

Tumbleweeds grow in America. When their seeds are ripe the plant curls into a ball. It rolls along in the wind, scattering the seeds.

The fastest seeds

The Squirting Cucumber plant fills up with water and squirts its seeds out. They travel at about 100km (60 miles) an hour.

Internet link *For a link to a Web site where you can read more about how seeds travel, go to* **www.usborne-quicklinks.com**

Roots and shoots

In the spring, days grow longer and warmer. Seeds get the warmth and rain they need to make them grow.

The seeds split and shoots grow up toward the light.

Roots grow down into the soil. Soon more roots will grow.

The roots feed the plant with water and goodness from the soil. They also hold the plant in the ground.

Leaves and sunlight

Little seed leaves feed the plant until the big leaves grow. Leaves have a special way of using air and sunlight to make plant food.

Growing beans

Put some wet kitchen roll in a jar with some water.

Put some beans next to the glass.

Put the jar in a warm, light place. The beans will swell up until they split and sprout roots and shoots.

Waterways

Plants suck up the water they need through their waterways. These are very thin tubes inside the stems.

Try this

You will need:
- a big jar
- some food dye
- some white flowers

In the soil

Worms pull leaves down into the soil.

Soil is full of things which are good for plants. Dead leaves, plants and tiny creatures rot away and make good plant food.

Put some water in the jar and add a few drops of food dye. Stand the flowers in it. After a few days the petal tips will change color.

In two more days, the flowers will be the same color as the dye. This is because the flowers suck the water and dye up into the petals.

Internet link For a link to a Web site where you can try a simple experiment to show how plants suck up water, go to **www.usborne-quicklinks.com**

207

Things you can grow

You can buy packets of flower and vegetable seeds in the shops. Here are some of the things you will need when you plant seeds for yourself.

– plant pots or yogurt cups
– a bag of compost
– a small watering can or jug
– a little trowel or an old spoon
– a plate
– some kitchen paper
– cress and sunflower seeds

Compost is a special soil with rich plant food in it.

Growing cress

Cress grows very easily and quickly at any time of the year.

Your cress will be ready to eat when it is about 7cm (3in) high.

You do not need soil, just some damp kitchen paper on a plate. Sprinkle some cress seeds on top.

Put the plate in a light place. The tiny shoots will soon grow, but you must keep the paper damp.

Sunflowers

In the spring you can start to grow sunflower seeds in pots.

Use a pot of compost for each seed. Push the seed in and sprinkle a little compost on top. Water the pots and put them in a warm, sunny place.

Try measuring the sunflowers to see how tall they grow.

After a few weeks shoots will appear and the plants will grow bigger. When they have four leaves they are big enough to plant in the garden.

Remember

Plants need these things to help them grow well.

They need sunlight to help them make their own special plant food.

They need water, but not too much, or they may rot.

They need soil because it gives them water and food.

Internet link For a link to a Web site where you can find out about flowers you can grow yourself, go to **www.usborne-quicklinks.com**

Where flowers grow

In the town

Gardens and parks are not the only places in towns where you might find flowers growing.

Some seeds are blown on to the roofs, where they grow.

Dandelion seeds get into the cracks in pavements.

The sowthistle grows in waste places and by the roadside.

Ivy-leaved toadflax grows on walls. It has purple flowers.

In the country

Many wild flowers grow in different countries all over the world. These flowers grow in Europe.

The red horse chestnut tree has groups of flowers.

The sweet briar has pink flowers and prickly stems.

The white dead-nettle has white flowers.

The flowers of the wild cherry tree smell very sweet.

In hot places

A cactus stores water in its stem.

In Australia, some flowers grow quickly after rain.

Desert plants have special ways of surviving without much rain.

In cold places

The edelweiss flower has a coat of fluff. It keeps the warmth in and the cold out.

Cushion pink grows close to the ground, out of the icy wind.

Plants which grow in cold, snowy places have ways of staying alive.

By the water

Some flowers grow well by the sea, by streams and other damp places.

Sea holly grows on beaches. It has spiky leaves and light blue flowers.

The marsh marigold likes ditches and wet places.

Sea bindweed has pink flowers with white stripes. It likes sandy beaches.

Water crowfoot floats on top of the water.

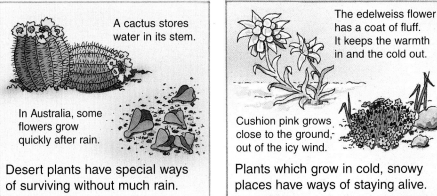

211

Amazing plant facts

Many strange plants and flowers grow in parts of the world. They are all sorts of amazing shapes and sizes. Some even eat small animals.

The biggest flowers

The rafflesia flower is also very smelly.

The flower of the rafflesia plant is the biggest flower in the world. It measures nearly 1m (3ft) across.

The giant cactus

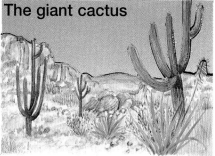

The saguaro is the largest cactus in the world. It grows as high as 15m (50ft) and lives for over 200 years.

Tiny plants

The smallest flowering plant is a kind of duckweed. It is so tiny that it looks like scum on the water.

*Internet link For a link to a Web site where you can learn more about the saguaro cactus, go to **www.usborne-quicklinks.com***

Flower traps

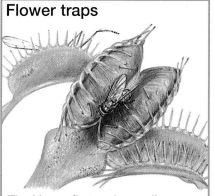

The Venus fly trap has spiky leaves. They snap shut to catch insects and tiny animals inside.

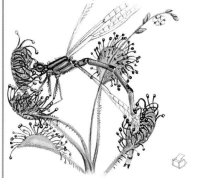

The sundew plant has leaves with sticky blobs. Insects stick to them and are eaten as plant food.

The oldest pot plant

A man grew a plant in a pot in Vienna in 1801. It is still alive today.

The strongest water lily

The victoria amazonica water lily is strong enough for a child to stand on its thick, floating leaves.

Internet link For a link to a Web site where you can find out more about Venus fly traps, and discover how to grow one, go to **www.usborne-quicklinks.com**

Useful words

You can find all of these words in this section of the book.

hay fever
People with hay fever sneeze when there is a lot of pollen in the air.

insect
This is a small animal with 6 legs and a body made of 3 parts. A bee is an insect and so is a butterfly and an ant.

nectar
This is sweet liquid food inside a flower. Small visitors come to drink it. Bees use it to make honey.

pistil
New seeds grow in this part of the flower. It is also called the seed box.

pollen
This is the name for tiny golden specks on a flower. It makes new seeds grow in another flower.

roots
These parts of a plant grow down into the ground. They take in water and goodness from the soil.

sepals
These wrap around a bud to keep it safe while it is growing.

shoots
These are the new parts of a plant.

stamen
This part of a flower has pollen at the end.

stem
This is the stalk of a plant. It holds the flowers up, above the ground.

stigma
This flower part is sticky. Pollen from another flower sticks to it easily.

waterways
These are thin tubes inside a plant stem. The plant drinks water through them, to stay alive and to grow.

Internet links

Go to **www.usborne-quicklinks.com** and type in the keywords "pocket scientist" for links to these Web sites about flowers and plants.

Web site 1 Help Detective Le Plant, Bud and Sprout unravel the mystery of plant life.

Web site 2 Learn about different kinds of plants and flowers and how they grow. You can try some experiments too.

Web site 3 Watch a movie about how flowers are pollinated.

Web site 4 Here you'll find lots of projects and activities involving plants and flowers.

Web site 5 There are lots of things to grow, do and make on this site about herbs. You can make a viewer to watch a seed grow.

Web site 6 Find out how to grow flowers and other plants. There is also advice about keeping your plants healthy and how to plan your garden.

Web site 7 Meet Squirmin' Herman, a cartoon worm, and find out why worms are important to plants and soil.

Web site 8 Find out all about bees and how they make honey.

Web site 9 Take a virtual tour of an amazing children's garden. You can explore a maze, visit a tree house and find plants that dinosaurs ate. You can also create a plant of your own.

For links to all these sites, go to www.usborne-quicklinks.com and type in the keywords "pocket scientist".

More Internet links

Here are some more Web sites to visit to find out about flowers and plants. For links to all these sites, go to **www.usborne-quicklinks.com** and type in the keywords "pocket scientist".

Web site 1 Watch a movie that explains how plants grow.

Web site 2 Find out about some of the many different types of plants found around the world.

Web site 3 The photographs and detailed descriptions in this field guide will help you to identify wild flowers.

Web site 4 Read about all kinds of poisonous plants and the effects they can have on people and animals.

Web site 5 Find out about the wonderful wild flowers that grow in Alaska.

Web site 6 Read about different types of seeds and find out how they are spread by the parent plant, then test your knowledge in the seed quiz.

Web site 7 Do you know whether a tomato is a fruit or a vegetable? Find out on this site, which explains the differences between fruits and vegetables.

Web site 8 Discover how to make compost and find out why it is so good for your garden.

Web site 9 Here you'll find a collection of photographs of plants and flowers that are free to download and use.

For links to all these sites, go to www.usborne-quicklinks.com and type in the keywords "pocket scientist".

WHAT MAKES IT RAIN?

Susan Mayes

Designed by Mike Pringle
Illustrated by Richard Deverell and Mike Pringle

Edited by Heather Amery
and revised by Philippa Wingate
With thanks to Katarina Dragoslavić

CONTENTS

All about rain

When gray clouds start to fill the sky, this often means that rain is on the way.

The rainwater runs down drains, or into streams, rivers and lakes. Some of it makes puddles on the ground.

Sometimes there is too much rain and sometimes there is not enough. When the air is cold, snow may fall.

When the rain stops and the sun comes out, puddles on the ground get smaller and smaller.

Where does the water go when it dries up? How does water get into the sky to make more rain?

What is a weather forecast and how is it made? You can find out about all of these things in this section.

Where the water goes

After a shower of rain, heat from the sun begins to dry up all the water on the ground.

The water turns into tiny droplets in the air, leaving the ground dry. The droplets are so tiny that you can't see them. They are called water vapor.

When the water dries up, this is called evaporation.

Try this

On a hot day, try this experiment to make water dry up.

Put two plates in a sunny place with a spoonful of water in each one.

Shade one plate with a book.

Look at the plates every hour.

Heating up

If a pan without a lid boils on high heat for a long time, the water evaporates and the food burns.

The water in the sun dries up first. Water always evaporates more quickly in the hot sun than it does in the cool shade.

Internet link For a link to a Web site where you can read more about evaporation and find out what causes dew and frost, go to **www.usborne-quicklinks.com**

Warm air

When the air is warmed, it rises. You cannot see it moving, but you can sometimes see how it takes things up, high into the sky.

Try this

Hold a very thin piece of tissue paper over a hot air heater.

Never let the paper get too close.

The air warmed by the heater rises and lifts the paper.

Smoke from a fire rises up the chimney and into the sky.

Warm air from a bonfire carries sparks and bits of ash upward.

The sun's heat

Warm air and water vapor

Air rises when it is warmed by the sun. It carries water vapor from the land and sea up into the sky.

221

Water in the air

When water vapor in the air cools, it turns into water drops which you can then see. This is called condensation.

Your warm, damp breath makes steamy clouds on a cold day.

Try this

Breathe hard on a cold mirror and see what happens.

The water vapor in your breath collects on the mirror and makes it mist up.

Steam from hot water is water vapor which has turned into tiny drops in the cold air.

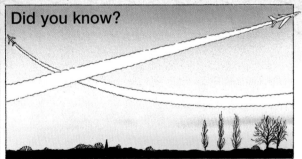

Did you know?

You can sometimes see water vapor very high in the sky behind airplanes.

It is pushed out of the engines and leaves a long trail of white clouds in the cold air.

Dew

On a warm day there is a lot of water vapor in the air. This is because warm air can hold more water vapor than the cold air.

As the warm air cools at night, some of its water vapor condenses. It turns into water drops on leaves and cool ground.

These water drops are called dew. You can see it on the ground in the early morning. The sun soon dries it up.

Frost

If the air gets very cold at night, dew freezes into frost.

Fog

Fog is lots of tiny water drops in the air. The drops form when air full of water vapor cools near the ground.

Sometimes it is so cold that dew does not form. Water vapor condenses straight into frost.

Frost is often so thick and white that it looks like a covering of snow on the ground.

Cold air

The heat from the sun bounces off the ground and warms the air near it. The air higher up in the sky is much colder. It is so cold that high mountain tops are snowy all year.

How clouds form

Every day water from the sea evaporates in the sun.

The warm air near the ground carries the water vapor up into the sky.

The cold air makes the water vapor condense into groups of tiny drops or ice crystals. We see them as clouds.

Did you know?

In some parts of the world people can sunbathe on a beach and see snow on the high mountains.

Above the clouds

When you take off in an airplane, you can go through the clouds and fly above them. The sun shines up there all the time during the day.

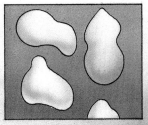

Inside a cloud

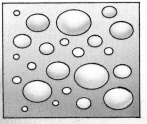 

The millions of tiny water droplets which make a rain cloud are different sizes.

Big drops fall and bump into smaller ones. They join and make bigger drops.

When the water drops are heavy enough they fall to earth as drops of rain.

Below the clouds

The rainwater collects in seas, lakes, rivers and puddles. When it stops raining the sun will start to dry up this water.

Snowy weather

How snowflakes form

Most water drops in high clouds freeze into tiny specks of ice in the cold air.

As they fall, more water freezes on them. They become ice crystals.

When the crystals are big enough, they join together and fall as snowflakes.

Falling snowflakes soften in warmer air. They stick together easily. Sticky snow makes good snowballs.

Snowflake facts

All snowflakes are a six-sided shape.

Millions of snowflakes have fallen to earth, but nobody has ever found two which are exactly the same.

People have seen huge snowflakes the size of large plates.

Avalanches

A skier or a loud noise can start an avalanche.

An avalanche is lots of snow which slides down a steep mountain slope. This may happen when the weather gets warmer and snow starts to melt.

Hail

Hailstones are hard lumps of ice which form inside a storm cloud. They fall to the ground very quickly in a hailstorm.

Raindrops freeze into ice pellets at the top of a storm cloud.

Air currents toss them up and down. More water freezes on to them.

When the pellets are too heavy to stay up, they fall as hailstones.

Inside a hailstone

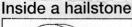

If you cut a hailstone you would see the layers of frozen water.

Did you know?

The biggest hailstone was 19cm (7½in) across, nearly as big as a soccer ball.

Hailstone damage

Big hailstones can make dents in cars and break windows. A bad hailstorm can flatten a field of corn in just a few minutes.

227

Rainbows

Next time it rains and the sun is shining at the same time, look for a rainbow.

How a rainbow is made

A ray of light looks white but it is really made up of many colors. When the sun shines through a raindrop the water splits the light into all its colors.

Sunlight

Raindrop

The colors bounce off the back of the drop and bend as they come out.

Rainbow colors

There are seven main colors in a rainbow and they are always in the same order – red, orange, yellow, green, blue, indigo and violet.

Try this

Put a glass of water on a sheet of white paper. Make sure it is in front of a sunny window.

When the sun shines brightly, a small rainbow will appear on the paper.

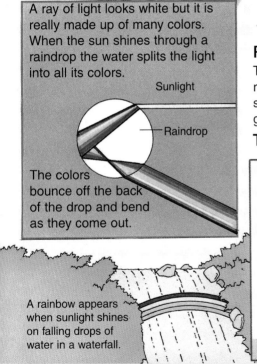

A rainbow appears when sunlight shines on falling drops of water in a waterfall.

Internet link For a link to a Web site where you can watch a video showing how rainbows are made, go to www.usborne-quicklinks.com

Thunderstorms

Tall, dark clouds often bring a storm with thunder and flashes of lightning.

What is lightning?

A kind of electricity, called static electricity, starts to build up in a storm cloud.

When there is too much, it jumps from the cloud in a huge, hot spark. This spark is the flash of lightning which you see in the sky.

Why do we hear thunder?

A flash of lightning heats the air around it very quickly. It starts a huge wave of air which grows bigger and bigger. This makes the thunder which you hear.

Lightning can go from cloud to cloud, or from the cloud down to the ground.

Try this

Make your own spark of static electricity. Press a large lump of modeling clay onto a metal tray to make a handle. Hold the modeling clay and rub the tray around on top of a thick plastic bag.

In the dark, hold something metal near the corner of the tray. Watch a spark jump away.

Internet link *For a link to a Web site where you can find out how to make your own thunderstorm, go to* **www.usborne.quicklinks.com**

229

Water on the ground

In a town, rainwater runs down the drains. It is carried away by underground pipes.

In the country, rainwater runs down slopes and into streams, rivers and lakes. Some soaks into the ground.

As a stream flows along, it is joined by more water from springs and from under the ground.

A river finds the easiest way across the land.

The water trickles down through the soil. It goes into underground streams and wells, then it travels on under the ground.

Sometimes underground water comes out of the side of a hill as a spring. Most streams start in this way.

Snow and ice melt when the weather warms up. The water runs away and soaks into the ground.

As the rivers, streams and springs make their way to the sea, some of their water evaporates.

More streams join together and they form a river.

A small river which flows into a bigger one is called a tributary.

Some water collects in hollows in the ground. This is how lakes are formed.

The river mouth is where the water runs out into the sea and ends its journey.

Water evaporates from the sea every day. The tiny invisible droplets will soon collect to make more clouds.

Internet link For a link to a Web site where you can read about how streams become rivers and see photographs of their different stages, go to **www.usborne-quicklinks.com**

231

Too much rain

A flood sometimes happens when there is a very heavy rainstorm, or if it rains for a very long time. The water cannot all seep away into the ground and it runs onto the land. Streams and rivers overflow with water.

Snow and ice

Floods sometimes happen in the spring when snow and ice start to melt. The water cannot soak into the soil because the ground is frozen hard underneath.

Stopping the water

A dam is a wall which is built across a river to make a lake. It holds the water back and can also be used to control floods.

A sudden flood

A flood which happens very suddenly is called a flash flood. It happens when a huge amount of rain falls in one place in a very short time.

There was a flash flood in New South Wales, Australia, in April 1989. The water swept away roads, bridges, cars, buildings and animals.

Living with rain

People in Indonesia build houses on stilts. They will be safe above the water when the floods come.

Moving away

The people of Barotseland, Zambia, move away when the floodwaters come. They take all their belongings to higher ground.

The driest places

Drought

In some places it does not rain for many weeks. There is not enough water to drink or to grow plants. This dry time is called a drought.

Did you know?

A strange plant grows in Africa's Namib Desert. Its leaves soak up water vapor from fog and it lives for a least a thousand years.

Deserts are the driest places in the world. In some places it does not rain for years. Any water evaporates quickly in the hot sunshine.

Cacti are desert plants which store the water they need in their stems.

In the United States, water from the Colorado River runs along canals to the Sonoran Desert. It is pumped onto the dry land to water crops.

The long roots of the mesquite plant find water 53m (174ft) under the ground.

Kangaroo rats never drink. Their bodies have a special way of making water from the dry seeds they eat.

Did you know?

A camel can live for as long as ten days in the desert without drinking.

Its body slowly turns fat in the hump into the water it needs.

Desert flowers

Seeds of flowers lie in the dry soil waiting for the rain. When it falls, the flowers bloom very quickly but they only live for a day or two.

What kind of weather?

A weather forecast tells you what the weather is going to be like. You can see it on television, hear it on the radio, or read it in the newspaper.

Weather forecasts can help you decide what to wear or where to go for the day.

People who need to know

An aircraft pilot needs to know what the weather will be like on the flight.

A fisherman needs to know if the weather at sea is going to be fine or stormy.

A farmer uses weather forecasts every day. He needs good weather for a lot of his work.

Making a weather forecast

A weather station is where facts about the weather are collected at certain times every day.

More facts come from satellites which study the weather from space.

They measure the wind speed and the water vapor in the air. They even measure the temperature.

Forecasters collect facts from weather stations around the world and from satellites. They use the facts to make weather charts.

They use these charts to help make a weather forecast. This tells you what the weather will be like over the next few days.

Useful words

You can find all of these words in this section of the book.

canal
This is a special waterway built for ships and to carry water across land.

condensation
This is tiny drops of water you see on cold things. It forms when warm damp air touches something that is cold.

desert
This is a dry place, where it hardly ever rains. Only a few plants grow.

dew
This is the name for the small drops of water which form on cool ground, leaves and plants.

evaporate
This is what happens when water dries up. It turns into tiny, invisible water drops in the air.

flood
This is when lots of water covers the land, after too much rain.

fog
This is tiny drops of water which you can see in the air. It looks like patches of low cloud.

frost
This is tiny drops of frozen water which appear on the ground and on other things in cold weather.

hail
This is the name of lumps of ice which form in a storm cloud.

water vapor
This is the name for tiny droplets of water in the air. The droplets are so small you cannot see them.

weather satellite
This is a machine sent into space to study the weather around earth.

Internet links

Go to **www.usborne-quicklinks.com** and type in the keywords "pocket scientist" for links to these Web sites about the weather.

Web site 1 Click on the maps to find out what the weather is like anywhere in the world.

Web site 2 Find out about the water cycle by following the adventures of Drippy the Raindrop from the sea to the clouds and back again.

Web site 3 Here you'll find fascinating information about all kinds of weather, from tidal waves to tornadoes.

Web site 4 Visit a meteorologist's own Web site and see pictures of him on air. You can read all about extreme weather conditions, listen to weather sounds and find lots of useful links to other Web sites.

Web site 5 Here you can find out how to make your own barometer in a bottle.

Web site 6 Read weather fact files, play games and try out weather projects. You can also find out how to become a weather forecaster.

Web site 7 Here you'll find information and activities, including building your own weather station and learning to read RADAR images.

Web site 8 Find out about hurricanes, tornadoes, floods and storms. Discover what to do to prepare for them and make sure you are safe. You can also test your knowledge in a quiz.

For links to all these sites, go to www.usborne-quicklinks.com and type in the keywords "pocket scientist".

More Internet links

Here are some more Web sites to visit to find out about the weather. For links to all these sites, go to **www.usborne-quicklinks.com** and type in the keywords "pocket scientist".

Web site 1 Watch a movie all about the water cycle and how rain is created.

Web site 2 Read people's real life weather stories and send in a story of your own.

Web site 3 Information about weather and climate. There's also a database to help you investigate the weather.

Web site 4 Watch a movie to find out all about thunder and lightning.

Web site 5 Read about why and how floods happen, plus real life flood stories and information about flood fighters.

Web site 6 Follow Hurricane Harry to find out how hurricanes are measured, where they occur and the damage they can do.

Web site 7 Read tips to help you keep safe in extreme weather, including tornadoes, lightning, flash floods and hurricanes.

Web site 8 Here you can find out all about snow and how it is formed. There are also games, quizzes, activities and advice on staying safe in the snow.

Web site 9 Use the chart on this Web site to identify different types of clouds. Photographs show you what each type looks like.

For links to all these sites, go to www.usborne-quicklinks.com and type in the keywords "pocket scientist".

WHERE DOES ELECTRICITY COME FROM?

Susan Mayes

Designed by Mike Pringle
Illustrated by John Shackell and John Scorey

Revised by Philippa Wingate
With thanks to Katarina Dragoslavić and Rosie Dickins
Series editor: Heather Amery

CONTENTS

Electricity at work

Electricity gives power, light
and heat to cities, towns and
villages all over the world.

Electricity makes street lights work
and powers a high-speed train.
242

It can travel long distances to
work in places far away.

You cannot see electricity but you can see where it is working around you, all the time.

How is electricity made? How does it get to your home and what can it do?

You can find out about all of these things in this section.

Electricity and light

The first electric light bulb was made by Thomas Edison in 1879. Now millions of them are used all over the world.

How many light bulbs can you count in and around your home?

Inside a light bulb

When you turn on a switch, electricity goes through the wires into the bulb.

It goes into a thin coil of wire, called a filament, and makes it heat up.

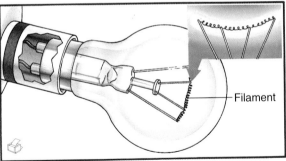

Filament

The filament is made of a metal called tungsten, which gets hot without melting.

It gets hotter and hotter until it glows white. This glow is the light you see.

Did you know?

Some lighthouses use lamps which are 20 times brighter than bulbs in your home.

Special mirrors make the light shine as far as 40km (24 miles) over the sea.

Electricity can be very dangerous. Never play with it.

Electricity and heat

Special wires which carry electricity heat up when the electricity flows through them.

Hot wires are very useful because they heat up all sorts of things.

An electric heater has heating wires inside. When electricity goes through them, they get hot and the heater warms the room.

Electricity heats coils of wire in a hairdryer. A fan blows air over the hot wires. This heats up the air so you can dry your hair.

On most electric cookers, each ring has a heating wire inside. The electricity flows through and heats the ring, so you can cook on it.

Did you know?

Some soccer fields have heating wires under the ground.

They stop the field from freezing when the weather is cold.

Never use anything electrical near water.

How a battery works

Some toys need a small amount of electricity to make them work. They get it from a battery.

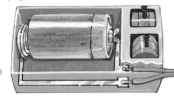

Inside the battery, special chemicals work together to make the electricity. It then travels through the wires to make the toy work. The battery stops working when the chemicals are used up.

Things which use batteries

Many watches use electricity from tiny, thin batteries.

A flashlight bulb lights up when electricity from the batteries passes through it.

A car has a special, powerful battery. Its electricity makes the engine, lights and heater work.

Try this

To light up a bulb you will need:
– 2 pieces of flex (wire covered with plastic)
– a 1.5 volt flashlight battery
– a 1.5 volt flashlight bulb
– a bulb holder
– sticky tape
– a small screwdriver
– a pair of scissors

1. Screw the bulb into the bulb holder.

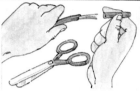

2. Strip off the plastic at each end of the wire.

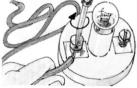

3. Fix the end of one wire to the bulb holder.

4. Fix the second piece of wire to the other side of the holder.

5. Use sticky tape to fix one piece of wire to each end of the battery.

6. Watch the bulb light up when the electricity passes through it.

Electricity which moves along a wire is called electric current.

If the current cannot go along its path, or circuit, the light goes off.

247

How a telephone works

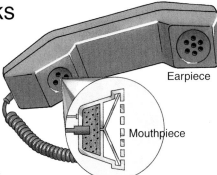

Earpiece

Mouthpiece

When you dial a number, an electric message goes to the telephone exchange. It tells the machine in the exchange which telephone to ring.

There is a microphone inside the mouthpiece. It changes the sound of your voice into electric signals which can be sent along cables.

Some cables go under the sea to take messages to other countries.

The person you are talking to hears you through the earpiece.

Some cables go overground but most go underground. The signals can travel great distances.

There is a tiny loudspeaker inside the earpiece. It changes the signals back into the sound of your voice.

About television

Electricity makes your television work as soon as you switch on. It brings you the pictures you see and the sounds you hear.

How it works

A television camera turns pictures into electric signals.

The microphone picks up sounds and turns them into more signals.

The signals travel along a cable to a television transmitter.

It sends the picture and sound signals through the air.

The television antenna on your house picks up the signals.

The television turns the signals back into pictures and sounds.

Did you know?

In space, machines called satellites can pick up electric signals from radios, telephones and televisions. They send them around the world.

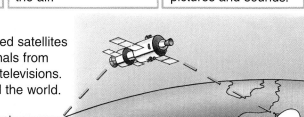

The signals are sent by a big transmitter.

Electricity to your home

Electricity is made in a power station. At the power station it is fed into a transformer.

The transformer makes the electricity stronger so lots of power can be sent to people who need it.

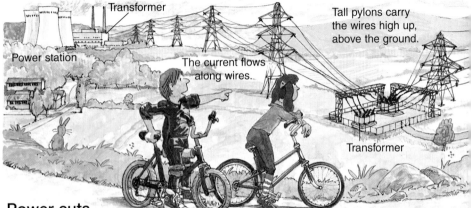

Transformer

Power station

The current flows along wires.

Tall pylons carry the wires high up, above the ground.

Transformer

Power cuts

Sometimes, lightning strikes a power line and damages it.

Circuit breakers stop electricity flowing along the broken part.

Some people have no electricity until the line is mended.

Electricity is fed around the country to other transformers. They make it weaker, so you can use it at home.

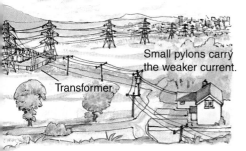

Small pylons carry the weaker current.

Transformer

Under the ground

In town, electric cables go under the ground. They bring the current into your home.

Workmen often dig up the road to repair the cables underneath.

In the house

The wires that carry power round your house are hidden safely in walls, in ceilings or under floors.

Plugging in

Electricity makes tools, lamps and electrical machines work anywhere you can plug them in.

The plug fits into a socket at the wall. When it is switched on, the electricity goes along the wire.

How electricity is made

The electricity which is used in your home
is made in different kinds of power stations.

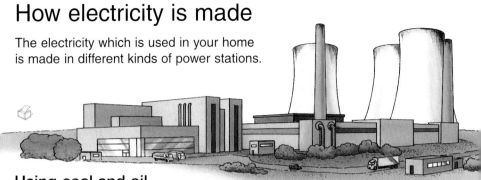

Using coal and oil

1. Coal and oil were made millions
of years ago, deep inside the Earth.
They are used in some power
stations to make electricity.

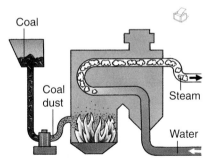

Coal

Coal
dust

Steam

Water

2. Coal or oil is burned in a boiler
to heat water. When the water gets
very hot, it turns into steam.

3. The steam goes along pipes to a
machine called a turbine. It pushes
against the metal blades and makes
them spin very fast.

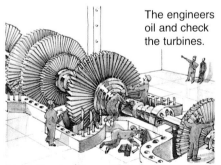

The engineers
oil and check
the turbines.

4. As the turbine spins,
it works a machine called a
generator. This makes the electricity.

252

Nuclear power stations

Nuclear power stations use fuel called uranium. It is dug out of the ground and used in a special way to make electricity.

The reactor

The uranium is made into rods. Inside the power station, they are put into the reactor. They are used to make heat.

Visitors can stand behind a window to look at the refueling machine.

Uranium sends out something dangerous which you cannot see, called radiation. A concrete shield around the reactor keeps it safe.

Water and steam

The heat made in the reactor boils water in pipes. This turns into steam which goes to the turbines.

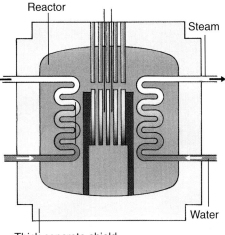

Reactor
Steam
Water
Thick concrete shield

The steam spins the turbines. They work the generator, which makes electricity like generators in other power stations.

Power from water

A hydro-electric power station uses falling water to make electricity. The water comes from a huge lake called a reservoir.

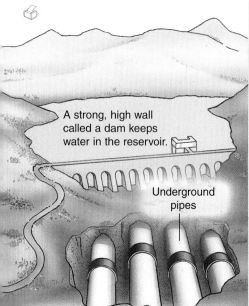

A strong, high wall called a dam keeps water in the reservoir.

Underground pipes

The water from the reservoir rushes downhill, through huge pipelines. Some are 10m (33ft) wide.

The turbines

At the bottom of each pipeline the water works the turbine runner.

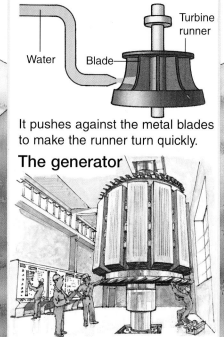

Water — Blade — Turbine runner

It pushes against the metal blades to make the runner turn quickly.

The generator

When the turbine runner spins, it works the generator and this makes the electricity.

Saving the water

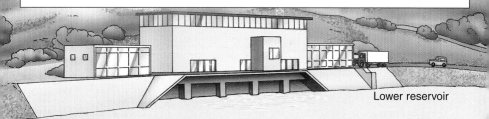

Top reservoir

Streams or rivers flow into the reservoir all the time and keep it full of water.

In hydro-electric power stations, the water flows away after it has been used to make electricity.

Lower reservoir

Some power stations save the water and use it again and again.

The water works the turbines, then it runs into a lower reservoir.

The pump

Electricity works huge pumps. They push the water back up to the top reservoir, ready to be used again.

Fishing

The water which has been used in the power station is clean. Fish can live in the reservoir.

Internet link *For a link to a Web site where you can take a look around a hydro-electric power station and click on different parts to find out how they work, go to **www.usborne-quicklinks.com*** 255

Going places

Electricity is used to work high-speed trains, subway trains, ships and airplanes. It even works the controls of space rockets.

Electric trains

Electric trains get electricity from overhead wires, or a third rail on the ground. It goes into motors which turn the wheels.

Overhead wires

This Japanese "bullet" train can travel up to 443km (227 miles) an hour.

Tracks and wires

Trolleybuses pick up electric current from overhead wires.

Some trams pick it up from an electric rail in a slot in the ground.

Subway trains are worked by electricity from extra rails.

On the sea and in the air

Electricity works special controls and instruments on ships and airplanes.

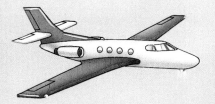

Electric circuits work dials and levers in an airplane.

A ship needs electricity to give light and heat. It is also used to work the radio and control the steering.

Space travel

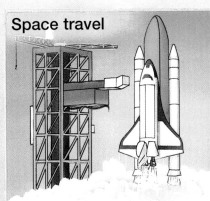

This space shuttle is fired into space by electric signals.

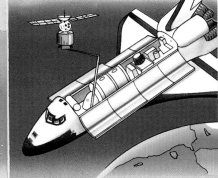

Electric circuits in a computer help the crew to fly the shuttle and work scientific instruments.

Other electricity

There is a kind of electricity called static electricity. It does not flow through wires like electric current, but it does some amazing things.

Try this

Rub a plastic pen on a woollen sweater for about 30 seconds.

Hold the pen very close to some small pieces of thin paper.

Watch the pieces of paper move toward the pen and stick to it.

Why it works

This works because static electricity builds up in the pen when you rub it against the wool.

It is the static electricity which pulls the paper toward the pen, making it jump, like magic.

Internet link *For a link to a Web site where you can discover what causes static electricity, go to **www.usborne-quicklinks.com***

Did you know?

Before a thunderstorm, static electricity builds up in storm clouds. When there is too much, it escapes as a flash of lightning.

Conductor

Tall buildings have a metal strip down the outside, called a lightning conductor.

If lightning strikes a building which has a conductor, it travels through the metal, down to the ground.

Tiny sparks

Lightning hit a tree during a storm in South Dakota, America.

Static electricity made the tree light up. Sparks twinkled on the end of each twig, like fairy lights.

Electricity in fish

Electric eels can make electricity in their bodies.

They stun their prey with electric shocks before eating it.

More power

One day, all the coal and oil which help make electrical power will be used up. Scientists have found other ways of making electricity.

Using the sun

Something called a solar panel can be put into your roof. It traps the sun's heat to warm the house.

Sunlight can make electricity using a device called a solar cell.

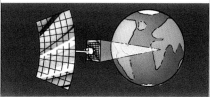

One day, scientists may put a solar collector, made of lots of solar cells, into space. The electricity made would be beamed to Earth.

Using the wind

The wind has powered windmills for hundreds of years. Now it is used to work special windmills which make electric power.

When the wind blows, it pushes against the huge blades and makes them turn. The moving blades work the generator to make electricity.

Using the waves

Scientists have worked out how to get power from the movement of waves, far out at sea. It makes electricity to use on land.

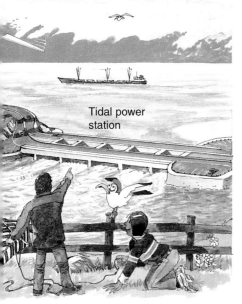

Tidal power station

Some countries have built tidal power stations. These make electricity using the flow of the tide, as it goes in and out.

High-speed travel

Some electric trains do not need wheels. They hover above special electric tracks.

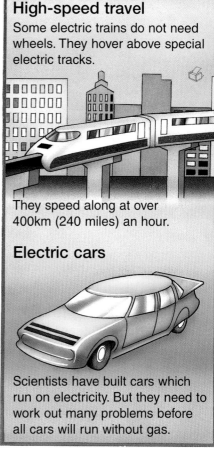

They speed along at over 400km (240 miles) an hour.

Electric cars

Scientists have built cars which run on electricity. But they need to work out many problems before all cars will run without gas.

Useful words

You'll find these words in this section.

antenna

This picks up electric signals from the air. If you have a television in your house, or a radio in your car, you need an antenna.

battery

This has special chemicals inside. They work together to make small amounts of electricity.

cables

These wires carry electric signals under the ground. They have a special covering to protect them.

circuit

This is a path of wires. Electricity must travel all the way round to work something electrical.

filament

This is the very thin coil of wire inside a light bulb. When electricity flows through, it glows brightly.

generator

This machine makes electricity. Huge generators make electricity in power stations.

pylons

These are strong, steel towers which carry electric wires safely, high above the ground.

reactor

This is the part of a nuclear power station where special fuel rods are used to make heat.

telephone exchange

This is where machines ring the telephone number you have dialed.

transformer

This changes the electricity to make it stronger or weaker.

turbine

This is a kind of machine which is worked by water, steam or air pushing against the blades.

Internet link For a link to a Web site where you can try a quiz about electricity safety, go to **www.usborne-quicklinks.com**

Internet links

Go to **www.usborne-quicklinks.com** and type in the keywords "pocket scientist" for links to these Web sites about electricity and where it comes from.

Web site 1 Here you'll find all kinds of information about energy and electricity, along with stories, puzzles and games. There's a super scientists gallery of energy pioneers, and ideas for your own energy experiments.

Web site 2 Lots of simple electricity experiments that you can do at home.

Web site 3 Explore the Energy Tree to see where electricity comes from.

Web site 4 Choose your spark level and then click on the pictures to find out how we use electricity around the home.

Web site 5 Read all about the history of electricity and the key inventions and discoveries.

Web site 6 Information about electric storms and lightning strikes, and how they are caused.

Web site 7 See where electricity comes from, get some electrical safety tips and find out how to read an electricity meter.

Web site 8 Louie the Lightning Bug explains all about electricity. You can find out what makes an electric eel electric, how our bodies use electricity, and how you can conserve energy and make your house energy efficient.

For links to all these sites, go to www.usborne-quicklinks.com and type in the keywords "pocket scientist".

More Internet links

Here are some more Web sites to visit to find out about electricity. For links to all these sites, go to **www.usborne-quicklinks.com** and type in the keywords "pocket scientist".

Web site 1 Find out how energy is made, learn about renewable energy and take a virtual tour of a power station. There are all kinds of energy-related activities to do too.

Web site 2 Watch a movie all about static electricity.

Web site 3 Watch a movie that explains how your television works.

Web site 4 Everything you need to know about how your television works, with photographs and detailed diagrams showing what it looks like inside.

Web site 5 Watch a movie that shows you how telephones work.

Web site 6 Read about Benjamin Franklin and his ground-breaking experiments about electricity.

Web site 7 Think about the things in your home that use electricity, and find out how to use them safely.

Web site 8 Find out about sources of natural energy, such as the sun, wind and water, and learn how we can use them.

Web site 9 An investigation into natural energy sources and their advantages and disadvantages.

Web site 10 Read some fascinating facts about the sun and solar energy.

For links to all these sites, go to www.usborne-quicklinks.com and type in the keywords "pocket scientist".

WHERE DOES TRASH GO?

Sophy Tahta

Designed by Lindy Dark
Illustrated by Colin King and Guy Smith

Edited by Cheryl Evans and revised by Philippa Wingate
Consultant: Chris Murphy

With thanks to Friends of the Earth,
Katarina Dragoslavić and Rosie Dickins

CONTENTS

All sorts of trash

You probably throw things away when they are old or broken or when you just don't want them any more.

But your trash is only a tiny part of the mountains of waste thrown out each year all over the world.

Garbage trucks collect trash from homes.

Trash is collected from schools, stores, hotels, offices and hospitals.

Waste comes from building sites, farms, factories and mines. Some is harmful and must be made safer.

Farm manure is kept in tanks and put on land to help things grow. It can harm rivers if it leaks into them.

A place to live

In some cities there are people who live in shacks called shanty towns. Many make a living selling scraps they find at trash dumps.

Shanty towns are made from junk materials such as scrap metal and wood.

Waste rock from mines is often covered with soil and sown with grass.

Find out more about different sorts of trash and what happens to them in this section.

Space junk

Millions of parts of spacecraft have been left in space. These could damage new craft going there. People need to clear up this junk.

Trash in the wrong place

Litter is trash that is dropped on the ground, into rivers or in the sea.

Clues to the past

People called archeologists study things which others once threw away or left behind, to find out about how they used to live.

Some of the things archeologists dig up are thousands of years old.

Ships throw tons of old nets and plastic trash in the sea each day, even though it's not allowed.

Sea litter can trap and choke turtles, seabirds, whales, fish and seals.

Broken glass and sharp cans left on the ground can cut animals.

You can help to stop litter from hurting animals or spoiling the view by putting yours in trash cans.

Not everything you throw away is trash. Notice the sorts of things you throw away each week. Most can be used again, as you will see.

267

Clearing up

Trash from stores, homes, schools, and so on is put into all sorts of bins or bags. These are collected and emptied into garbage trucks which crush the trash to pack more in.

Places such as schools or stores put trash in big, plastic or metal trash cans with wheels. Some homes do too.

Garbage trucks carry trash from hundreds of bins and bags.

This truck is filled up and emptied several times a day.

This is called a packer blade. It slides down, scoops trash into the truck and squeezes it against a panel.

Lots of trucks are fitted with special lifts. These lift up and tip out bins of all sizes.

Trash can lids keep smells and trash in and animals out.

This powerful machinery could be dangerous if you get too near.

As more trash is crammed in, this panel slides back to make more room.

Trash must be collected often or it can start to rot and attract rats and flies which spread diseases.

Cleaning the street

All sorts of machines are used to clean roads. In some places a street cleaner also sweeps pavements and empties trash cans into a cart.

This hose can be used to suck up dead leaves and litter.

This pipe sucks trash into the truck through a wide nozzle.

Nozzle

Strong brushes wash and scrub the road.

Water is sprayed out of holes in the nozzle and brushes.

People who collect trash and clean streets start early when roads are clear. Some even work at night.

Special collection

Venice in Italy has canals for streets. Trash is collected there by barges.

In cities such as Paris, in France, special scooters suck dog mess into a box with a hose.

Everest is the highest mountain in the world.

So much litter has been left on Mount Everest, that a team of climbers has been to pick it up.

269

On the move

In many towns, garbage trucks dump their trash at a place called a transfer station. From here it goes to big holes in the ground called landfills.

Tipped out

At some transfer stations, trash is tipped straight into a machine called a compactor.

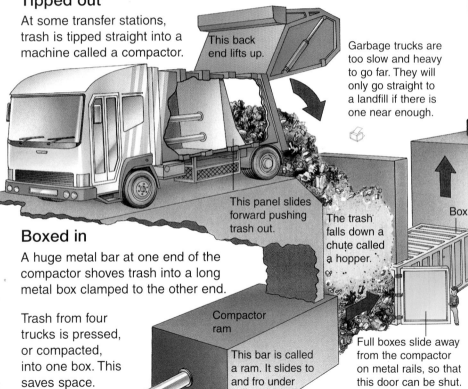

This back end lifts up.

Garbage trucks are too slow and heavy to go far. They will only go straight to a landfill if there is one near enough.

This panel slides forward pushing trash out.

The trash falls down a chute called a hopper.

Box

Boxed in

A huge metal bar at one end of the compactor shoves trash into a long metal box clamped to the other end.

Trash from four trucks is pressed, or compacted, into one box. This saves space.

Compactor ram

This bar is called a ram. It slides to and fro under the hopper.

Full boxes slide away from the compactor on metal rails, so that this door can be shut.

270

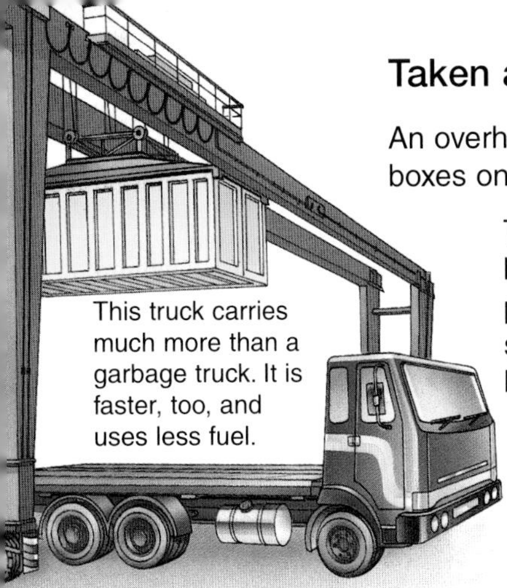

Taken away

An overhead crane lifts the boxes onto long, flat trucks.

Trains and barges may be used to carry boxes part of the way. Then special trucks take the boxes on to the landfill.

Not all stations cram trash into boxes, as shown here. Some load it straight into open-topped trucks.

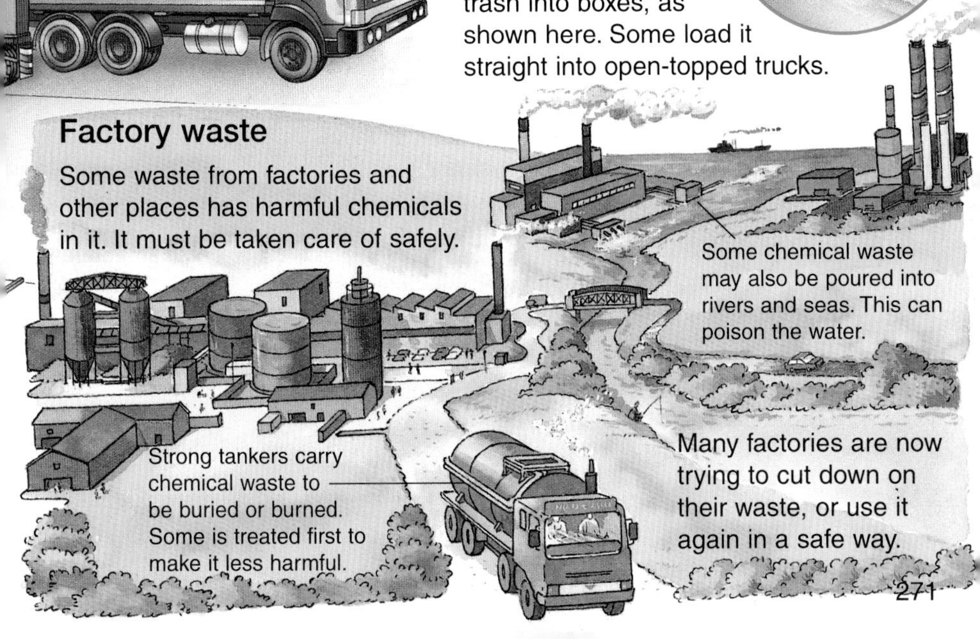

This truck carries much more than a garbage truck. It is faster, too, and uses less fuel.

Factory waste

Some waste from factories and other places has harmful chemicals in it. It must be taken care of safely.

Some chemical waste may also be poured into rivers and seas. This can poison the water.

Strong tankers carry chemical waste to be buried or burned. Some is treated first to make it less harmful.

Many factories are now trying to cut down on their waste, or use it again in a safe way.

271

Rotting away

Each day tons of trash are tipped out at landfills, crushed into layers and buried. Some of it rots away.

This truck tips up its box to let trash fall out.

A machine called a toothed-wheel compactor presses trash into layers.

Rotting food

Vegetable and garden waste rots into a rich muck called compost.

Many people make their own compost to help things grow. It is also made at a few special waste centers which sort food waste with machines.

The trash is covered with soil at the end of each day to keep litter and smells in and seagulls, rats and flies out.

These heavy wheels and spikes help to flatten the trash.

A shovel scoops up and spreads trash.

Some landfills are made in old quarries which are no longer used.

Buried dangers

Rainwater seeping through buried trash can turn into a poisonous ooze called leachate.

Leachate is harmful if it leaks through the soil into rivers or underground waterways.

A sloping clay cover over full cells lets rain run into side drains, instead of through the landfill.

Some landfills have a plastic or clay lining to keep leachate in. Leachate may be pumped out, too.

Most landfills are built up bit by bit in parts called cells.

Clay cap

Drain

Lining

Cell

Blow up

Rotting trash also makes a gas called methane which can explode if lit. In 1986, some leaked into a house in Britain. It was lit by a spark and blew up. Luckily, no-one was killed.

Heat up

Methane gas can be pumped out of landfills and used safely to make electricity, or to heat homes, brick ovens and even greenhouses.

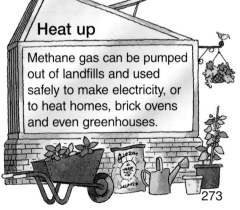

273

Up in flames

In big cities, trash may be burned in a place called an incinerator. This saves space in landfills, but gives off harmful gases, too.

1. Down the pit

Garbage trucks tip trash straight into a deep pit at the incinerator.

A person in a control room works the crane.

This grab crane moves along beams and lifts up and down.

2. Into the furnace

A crane grabs trash out of the pit and drops it down a chute into a giant oven called a furnace.

274

3. Burning up

The furnace must be terribly hot to make sure the trash burns properly and gives off fewer harmful gases.

Hot air, gas and smoke go this way.

Furnace

Air is blown over and under the trash to make it burn well.

Ash goes this way.

This sloping floor is called a grate. Moving rollers on top carry the burning trash along.

These rollers turn and break up the trash to make it burn better.

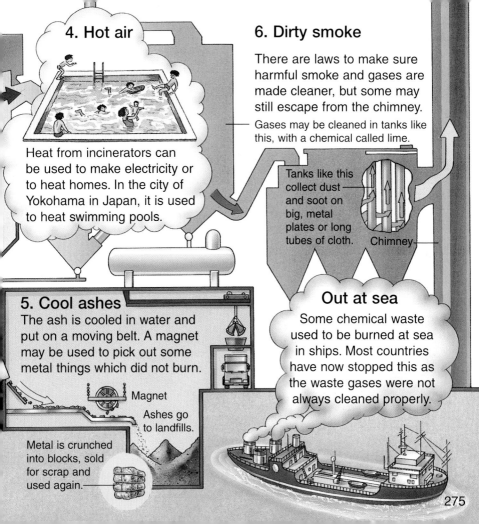

4. Hot air

Heat from incinerators can be used to make electricity or to heat homes. In the city of Yokohama in Japan, it is used to heat swimming pools.

6. Dirty smoke

There are laws to make sure harmful smoke and gases are made cleaner, but some may still escape from the chimney.

Gases may be cleaned in tanks like this, with a chemical called lime.

Tanks like this collect dust and soot on big, metal plates or long tubes of cloth.

Chimney

5. Cool ashes

The ash is cooled in water and put on a moving belt. A magnet may be used to pick out some metal things which did not burn.

Magnet

Ashes go to landfills.

Metal is crunched into blocks, sold for scrap and used again.

Out at sea

Some chemical waste used to be burned at sea in ships. Most countries have now stopped this as the waste gases were not always cleaned properly.

275

Down the drain

Each time you take a bath or flush the toilet, the waste water runs down the drainpipe to underground pipes called sewers. These take it to a place called a sewage works.

Sewage works help to keep rivers clean.

Internet link For a link to a Web site where you can find out about saving water, go to **www.usborne-quicklinks.com**

This bend is always full of water to stop smells from coming back up.

Drainpipes

Rainwater often runs down drains into sewers.

Inside pipes take waste to drainpipes outside.

Waste in sewers is called sewage.

Sewers from homes join bigger ones under the street. These join giant sewers which go to the sewage works.

Sewers run downhill if possible. Sewage is pumped along uphill pipes.

By the sea

In some seaside towns, sewage pours out of a long sewer pipe into the sea. It may be cleaned a little first, but often it is not.

This raw sewage can make the sea horrid to swim in.

In the country

In some homes in the country, sewage goes to underground tanks. Every year or so it is pumped out by a tanker and taken to a sewage works.

This shows a septic tank.

These pipes let some liquid drain slowly into the soil.

276

At the sewage works

Sewage flows through many tanks at the sewage works. These take out different things to make it cleaner.

1. This screen traps wood, rags and other large things.

2. Grit sinks to the bottom of this tank and is pumped out.

3. The sludgy part sinks down in this tank. From here sewage water and sludge go to different tanks.

Sewage water

Sewage sludge

4. Sewage water goes here, where it is mixed with a special liquid. This liquid has lots of tiny, living things called bacteria in it. These feed on dirt in the water and help to clean it.

6. Sewage sludge goes here, where bacteria in the sludge turn some of the dirt into methane gas. This gas can be used to run the works.

7. The thickest sludge sinks down here, leaving water on top. It is spread on land, burned or dumped at sea. Many countries have now stopped dumping it at sea.

5. The special liquid is pumped out of this tank and used again. The water goes into rivers.

277

Dangerous waste

Waste which poisons water, soil or air is called pollution. There are laws to stop people from causing pollution, or to make them pay to have it cleaned.

In the rivers

Waste from sewage works and farms can pollute rivers with chemicals called phosphates and nitrates.

Phosphates come from sewage and cleaning liquids and powders.

Nitrates are added to land to help things grow. Some wash into rivers.

These chemicals help to make too many plants called algae grow.

Algae use up air and light needed by other plants and animals.

In the sea

Oil tankers can pollute seas if they leak, or if they break the law and wash out their tanks at sea.

Oil clogs up birds' wings and chokes fish.

Oil spills are expensive and difficult to clean.

This nuclear power station uses nuclear power to make electricity.

Below ground

Some waste from nuclear power stations can be dangerous for thousands of years. It must be looked after very carefully.

Some nuclear waste is set in concrete and sealed in drums and boxes. These will one day be stored deep underground.

Acid rain

Waste gases from cars, factories and power stations pollute the air and some can turn rain sour, or acid. More gases could be cleaned before leaving chimneys.

Acid rain poisons trees and lakes.

It also wears away statues and buildings.

Car fumes

Car fumes make a poisonous, chemical smog when the sun shines on them. They can also send out lead, which is harmful to breathe.

A filter called a catalytic converter is fitted in car exhausts to clean gases which make smog and acid rain.

Most drivers use gasoline without any lead in it.

Greenhouse gases

Some waste gases trap heat in the air like the glass of a greenhouse. This could warm up the earth, causing parts of it to dry up. People need to stop making so many of these gases.

Heat escaping into space

Heat from the sun

Heat trapped by greenhouse gases

Greenhouse gases in the air above the earth

The ozone layer

The ozone layer is a layer of gas around the earth which protects living things from harmful sun rays. Gases called CFCs break down this layer.

Some CFCs are used in old refrigerators.

Using things again

Using trash again is called recycling. This saves using up so many things from the ground, called raw materials, to make new things. One day, some of these raw materials will run out.

Here are some things you can save which can be recycled, or used again.

Lots of this trash has been used to wrap or pack things. Using less packaging would make less trash.

Clothes, toys, books, old stamps and coins, can go to thrift stores, which can sell them again.

Food and garden waste can be turned into compost.

No waste

In Cairo, the capital city of Egypt, trash is collected by a group of people called the Zabaleens.

Trash is sorted and sold to people who can use it again.

Paper, bottles, cans and rags can be made into new things. Plastic can also be recycled in this way.

Internet link For a link to a Web site about recycling, go to *www.usborne-quicklinks.com*

Paper chain

Saved waste paper and cardboard goes to a paper merchant's yard. Here it is sorted, pressed into bales and sent to a paper mill for recycling.

At the mill, the paper is soaked in tanks of hot water and whisked into a mush called stock.

A machine spreads the stock onto a moving wire mesh to make paper.

The paper is fed onto a band of felt, which moves around different rollers.

Make your own paper

Try recycling your own paper.

Internet link For a link to a Web site about making paper, go to **www.usborne-quicklinks.com**

Soak torn bits of newspaper overnight in a little water. Mash it with a fork.

Drain it. Roll it with a rolling pin and let it dry.

Trim the edges and paint it. You could use your paper as a table mat.

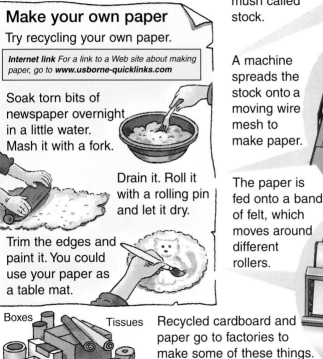

As the stock drains, thread-like fibers join up to make a big sheet of paper.

Pumps underneath suck water out.

Heavy rollers squeeze water out of the paper.

Hot rollers dry it.

Polished rollers smooth it.

This roller winds it into a reel.

Boxes

Tissues

Recycled cardboard and paper go to factories to make some of these things.

Newspapers

More things to save

Recycling also saves energy. Energy comes from burning fuels such as oil. It takes much less energy to recycle things, such as cans and bottles, than it takes to make new ones from scratch.

Sorting cans

Cans are made from different metals which can be melted down and used again. Use a magnet to see which metal yours are made from.

Hold the magnet to the side.

Most cans are made from steel which sticks.

Steel cans are picked out at some transfer stations with giant magnets.

Many drinks cans are made from aluminum which does not stick.

Recycling aluminum cans saves almost all the energy it takes to make new ones.

Less pollution

Recycling also cuts down on pollution from incinerators, landfills and mines, as less trash is burned or buried and fewer raw materials are dug up. This makes the countryside look nicer, too.

Saving bottles

Limestone

Soda-ash

Sand

Any old jars and bottles you save for recycling can be melted down with these other things at a glass factory, to make new ones.

Old glass can make up to half the amount. Using this much saves the most energy.

282

Internet link For a link to a Web site with recycling word games, go to **www.usborne-quicklinks.com**

Sorting trash

In many places, you can take your old newspapers, bottles and cans to special trash cans in the street, called banks.

Can bank

Paper bank

Bottle banks

A few banks take plastic bottles, too.

Money back

In some places, people pay a bit more for bottled goods in stores. They get this money back when they return the empty bottles.

Some countries have machines which give a coin for each aluminum can put in.

Sorting at home

In some places, people sort their trash into different trash cans or bags at home, to be collected separately.

In parts of Germany, food scraps are put into one trash can and collected separately to make compost.

Sorting centers

In some countries, jumbled-up trash is taken to a special waste center to be shredded and pressed into pellets.

These pellets are burned in factories as a fuel.

Big things

Sometimes people need to get rid of things which are too big to go in the trash can. They may be able to have them collected on special days, or they may take them to a recycling center.

These centers have huge, metal crates for people to put things in. Many have recycling banks, too.

This crate is for garden waste.

Rag bank

Old clothes can be made into new things such as blankets.

Battery bank

Metal things may be put in a separate crate and sold to a metal merchant for recycling.

This tank collects old car oil to clean and use again. Pouring oil down drains or on the ground is not allowed, as it can seep into rivers.

Batteries have harmful acids in them which can leak. They can be recycled.

Fly-tips

Dumping trash in places where it should not be is called fly-tipping. This spoils the towns and countryside.

Full crates are collected by trucks. Anything that cannot be recycled goes to a landfill.

Some rubble from building sites gets fly-tipped, even though this is not allowed.

On the scrap heap

Many old cars end up in a scrapyard. Here they are taken apart and crushed by powerful machines.

Useful things, such as engines, may be taken out and sold as spare parts.

This crane lifts the cars into a machine which flattens them.

Trains and planes

Scrap steel from old bridges, ships, trains and planes is also melted down to make more things.

The squashed cars go to a big scrap yard to be shredded into tiny bits of steel. These bits are melted down at a steel works.

Old batteries

The plastic cases and lead metal plates from car batteries can be recycled, too.

Used tires

Tires are difficult to bury or burn. People are always trying to find more ways to recycle them.

285

In the past

For thousands of years, most people lived in small, farming villages. They did not have as much as many people have now and they wasted very little.

Rotten fence posts were used for firewood.

Food scraps were fed to animals.

Food waste, ash, animal manure and sewage may also have been used to make compost.

Broken tools and clothes were mended.

Toilets in the past

Some castles had tiny rooms in the walls with a hole for a toilet. The waste fell down a chute into the moat or a pit.

These rooms are called garderobes.

About 500 years ago many people in towns used chamber pots, and tipped them out into the street below.

The first flush toilet was made in Britain in 1589 by Sir John Harington, but it was ages before most people had one.

Some rich people had really grand flush toilets.

Internet links

Go to **www.usborne-quicklinks.com** and type in the keywords "pocket scientist" for links to these Web sites about waste and recycling.

Web site 1 Learn about where garbage goes and what to do with hazardous waste.

Web site 2 Read about water pollution, clean up a virtual oil-spill and see what happens when you flush the toilet.

Web site 3 Puzzles and activities about trash and recycling.

Web site 4 Play a game where you have to stop toxic waste from flooding the landfill.

Web site 5 Learn all about water supplies, and what happens to waste water, through games and a water workshop.

Web site 6 Find out how you can reduce, reuse and recycle waste and help the environment.

Web site 7 Read these simple hints and tips for keeping our planet healthy.

Web site 8 Find out all about recycling and hazardous waste. You can also take the Salmon Challenge, where decisions you make will help or harm the environment and affect your salmon's chance of survival.

Web site 9 Lots of activities to help you learn about recycling, including making bird feeders out of household waste.

For links to all these sites, go to www.usborne-quicklinks.com and type in the keywords "pocket scientist".

Index

Cover design by Russell Punter and cover illustration by Christyan Fox. With thanks to Stephanie Turnbull.

First published in 2002 by Usborne Publishing Ltd., Usborne House, 83-85 Saffron Hill, London EC1N 8RT, England. www.usborne.com
Copyright © 2002, 2001, 1992, 1991, 1989 Usborne Publishing Ltd. The name Usborne and the device ♀ 🎈 are Trade Marks of Usborne
Publishing Ltd. All rights reserved. No part of this publication may be reproduced, stored in a retrieval system, or transmitted in any
form or by any means, electronic, mechanical, photocopying, recording, or otherwise, without the prior permission of the publisher.
AE. Printed in China.